3800 19 0013014 1

HIGH LIFE HIGHLAND

K.D.N.

D0581705

Last Chance in Laredo

Sometimes the past catches up with a man and he can't outrun it. Jack Brady, at just thirty years old, has seen more of the hard edge of life than most. He's worked cattle trails, ridden shotgun, and won a reputation as a hired gun. Then, as the American-Mexican War is breaking out, he is jailed after a fight in a small Texas town.

Brady is at his lowest when a preacher arrives and reminds him that there is still a chance to redeem himself and to honour his dead father. He determines to enlist with the fledgling Texas Rangers and joins Robert Gillespie's rough riders as they ride into Laredo.

But Brady has a man on his tail who is bent on revenge. And he faces the kind of trouble a woman can bring when she has to be protected. This is one last chance to rub out his bad reputation, if he can survive – but not many Rangers do that.

Last Chance in Laredo

Frank Callan

A Black Horse Western

ROBERT HALE

© Frank Callan 2019
First published in Great Britain 2019

ISBN 978-0-7198-2965-9

The Crowood Press
The Stable Block
Crowood Lane
Ramsbury
Marlborough
Wiltshire SN8 2HR

www.bhwesterns.com

Robert Hale is an imprint
of The Crowood Press

Typeset by
Derek Doyle & Associates, Shaw Heath
Printed and bound in Great Britain by
4Bind Ltd, Stevenage, SG1 2XT

1

He was settled in the corner of the saloon, happy to be left alone with his thoughts and the pains of the long ride through a stretch of land more like an oven than any kind of territory. He had no real notion of where he was heading, and he had ridden hard to make himself well clear of a bunch of folks who claimed they were kin of a man he had beaten up in some run-down collection of shacks they tried to call a town.

At that moment, life had nothing better to offer him than that little refuge, where he could be entertained by watching fools part with their dollars and women do their best to sweeten the disposition of lonely men. You had no need to think in a place like that: you were no more than a nameless stranger who drifted in like blades of grass pushed by the wind.

Whoever put that place together was weak on

imagination as well as wealth, calling it Short Bend. But right now it had food and drink and somewhere to rest his aching body. No faces in the crowd recognized him: he had the comfort of knowing that, as far as he knew, not a soul in that joint had a claim on his time or his services.

The second cool beer was easing the ache in his knees and back. Maybe Short Bend was not such a disappointment after all. But a rasping voice cut through the hum of relaxed conversation in the half-full bar.

'You're Jack Brady, and I'm here to get even.'

The speaker was so long and scrawny that a man could get a pain in the eyeballs looking up at his grizzled, hairy face. He wore a long grey coat and had a bandana tight up to his chin. So much for being left in peace. The man had his name right. There was maybe trouble coming.

'I might be. Who's asking, mister?'

'So you don't see Evan Wate looking down at you? Your eyes gone or somethin'? I followed you all the way from the Gulf. Now here we are in Texas, still fightin' for its place in the world. You happen to recall a small town called Nelland, Louisiana?'

'Nope. Reckon I don't. I seen a lot of small towns.'

'Well, you happen to recall a girl named Marie, in Nelland, Louisiana?'

'Lot of girls named Marie. Most common name in the world.'

'You're making my arms shake with the kind of

anger I try to avoid, mister.' The tall man said, with a dark threat.

Wate had no weapon visible. He slowly put his two fists out and gave his challenge. 'Come on, Brady, you ruined my little sister! Gentlemen. . . .' He looked around the room at all the faces, now turned on him and Brady. 'This here man, he's one for the ladies . . . oh yeah . . . he charms them with all that sweet talk like they expect and then he runs off and disappears. But now he's got a big brother in front of him. C'mon Brady!'

Jack Brady had his legs stretched out, real comfortable, and the beer had him in a good mood, but it looked like he was going to have to move. 'Mr Wate, you gone and did something inexcusable. You spoiled my day. Here we are, close on San Antonio, where I'm heading, and I'm feeling homely and warm. Then you come in, spoiling for a fight. I never seduced no sister of yours. I reckon you got me confused with Square John. He has a look of me I do say, and I hung out with him for a time down your way . . . the Gulf. I like to be by the sea.'

'Quit the little boy talk and stand up. Now you're lyin' to wriggle off the hook like a stuck trout.' He moved closer, letting both fists jut up to show his threat. Still Jack never moved at all.

Wate decided to act, and it was a big mistake. He kicked Jack's outstretched legs, savagely. It was a matter of seconds before Jack sprang forward and hit the tall man hard in the belly. He folded, and an uppercut hit him so hard he squealed and keeled over. But Jack didn't go for him; he let him struggle to his feet. Wate managed a blow on Jack's cheek, and in return he was grabbed, held and then thrown back at the bar counter, where he cracked his skull hard.

Jack Brady was six feet in his boots and muscled like an ox from his cow-poking days. He always lived with the saying that the bigger they are, the harder they fall, and he now rammed his head into Wate's gut, following up with a punch to the kidneys.

As Wate went down, Jack was suddenly aware of shouting and the noise of the crowd on the move. He felt arms tighten around him, and three men gripped him tight, as a man with a star on his shirt whipped the cuffs on Jack's wrist. 'Brady . . . you've a room for the night. Think you been there before. It still stinks of you!'

The next morning, Jack woke up in the sawdust and rodent droppings in Sheriff Mosey Digby's jail. He felt like his jaw was loose, and his head hurt like a hammer had smacked him hard.

Was this what life was about then? he was asking himself, as he stared at bugs walking across the planks, which were already adorned by rat droppings and the stink of stale food. Was this the kind of life he had dreamed of when he first hit out on his own for the next horizon?

Mosey was at his desk, drinking coffee in between scooping up beans and egg. 'This is real good, Brady. My wife takes such care of me . . . shame you never got no good woman. You was here a year back . . . drunk and violent. One of my men knows you from Kansas, too. He says you was trouble. Do you always provoke men twice your size?'

'When they lie I do.' Jack gave a wry smile.

'How many years are you draggin' around, old friend?'

'Thirty next April. T'ain't aged. Time yet, for settling I mean.'

Mosey finished his breakfast, wiped his mouth and stood up. He poured Jack some coffee and walked his solid, squat body across the room. He was most folks' idea of a wrestler. His muscles had run to fat but he looked like he could down a young steer, so strong and thick were his arms. He was bearded, rough and direct in everything. Pushing forty-five, he was the family man that Short Bend needed in charge.

'Brady, I've something to tell you. Now don't get all fired up. Fact is, there's a preacher coming along to see you. He asked me specially to let him help my customers. Killers was his choice but I told him you was no more than a public nuisance. He should be here soon . . . drink this coffee and then try to be civil to him . . . he's just a striplin' . . . maybe twenty-three years, lookin' more like ten!'

'I've no time for God, Sheriff Digby. Life's full

enough without packing no God in the bedroll. You let Him in, there's things stirred up in every second of your day. Anyway, the man up there over the clouds, he let me down.' He drank his coffee while Digby went back to his desk and shuffled some papers.

It was this low point in the course of his life that sent Jack Brady into the kind of thinking a man does when something inside is telling him that he's nearer than a horse's stride to a dead end. His mind went roving through the past, putting words and scenes before him that told him how he had wasted so much. *You're crowding thirty and still like a stray wolf digging in dirt,* he said to himself. There was the life of Jack Brady, set out before him like some cheap obituary in a Death County newspaper. Jack the runaway from the family of a failed medical man; Jack the hired hand, the shotgun-carrier, the too keen lawman, and then the drifting, no-good gun for hire. It was not a life that was leading anywhere in particular, but a midnight drinker on the Gulf had said, 'Go to San Antonio. They're looking for young fools like you,' and here he was, lost in every way except knowing he was in Short Bend, looking hard at jailhouse bars and trail-end failure.

It was as these thoughts plagued him that a voice asked, 'Are you the troublemaker from last night? I'm Pastor Jim.'

Jack looked up to see a man who surely lived for

10

food. He was what his pa used to call a grease-tub, coping with double-chins and timber limbs. He was not in sombre black, but in a worn-out cream dandy suit like some Southern gambler, and he spoke like an English gentleman.

'Pastor Jim – you mean, you're coming here selling God and paradise? I thought you monkish types lived on cabbage and air . . . you look like a seasoned trencherman to me.' Jack couldn't hide his contempt.

'No, I do not sell anything, Sir. I'm young, yes, but I'm wise enough to know that our Maker does not bully folk into signing up into His ranks. As to my build, well the Lord provides food and it needs to be shifted! Mind if I sit down, Sir?'

'Find a chair. If you ain't sermonizing then we're easy.'

Jack waited until the man pulled a chair across, then the preacher sat and looked searchingly into Jack's face. Meeting a man's look eye-to-eye was something Jack Brady had done a thousand times, but it had always been to sound out a sign of fear. This man never flinched, and his look suggested that he was someone who was a stranger to fear.

'Your name is Jack Brady, I'm told. That's a good, sound Saxon name. You look like I could rely on you if we were in trouble.' The pastor grinned, expecting a response, but nothing came, until Jack filled the silence with, 'I can be a good friend, but I'm cut out to ride alone.'

'Son, I've seen plenty of lost souls, and if I may speak direct and honest, you fall into that category. My work is to help such men find their true direction. See, we have a destiny. You give any credence to destiny, Jack Brady?'

'My destiny is in the lawman's lock-up cupboard . . . my gun and my knife.'

Pastor Jim nodded and took some time to consider. 'You are a man of violence then. I see all the signs. You're restless as a worker ant but you have nothing to build. Want to build something, Sir, something like a man's honour?'

Jack wanted to order the man out and to stop troubling him with fancy speech, but the word *honour* went deep. His father, though drink took him, had once been a man who talked about 'making a good name'. He had said so many times in his drunken monologues, 'Jack, make a good name for yourself . . . be honourable and be remembered. Don't let the grape seduce you, like your sad excuse for a father.'

'What is a man's honour, Pastor Jim?'

The fat man said, 'Proving you are a complete man, civil, and with a sense of right, and with a conscience.'

'Is it always a Godly thing then?'

'No. Finding it and winning it usually has means and ends. Like the outfit I'm travelling to . . . the Rangers. You could be a Texas Ranger, my friend. You could find honour with them, but they do win

12

their honour through questionable means. They write their honour in blood. You could help them keep the Mexicans out of their land . . . this land of wonderful optimism. I'm heading there because there's death everywhere, and men need comfort when they face it. You are tough enough to be a fighting *tejano*.'

'For a young man, you talk a lot, and you talk old . . . why are you going to them?'

'I've been asked for, by an old friend of my uncle's . . . he's a sick man. He tells me that there's big trouble brewing and the Rangers are helping the army. Fact is, my friend, they don't live long, these men. That's at the back of their minds every time they move out for action.'

Now Jack knew what the man down in East Texas meant when he said they were looking for young fools over in the west, across along the borderland. He had an inkling that the pastor was talking sense. Never in his life had he listened to a sermon, but there was something about Pastor Jim that was different. He woke a mix of fear and guilt in a man.

'Well, Jack Brady . . . I could use a guard on my trip . . . though it's not so far,' Pastor Jim said.

The pastor could see that he had said enough now and he stuck an arm through the bars, shook hands with Jack and walked towards the door, nodding at the sheriff. But words went through Jack's mind again: you can find honour with your gun.

13

Maybe, Jack thought, the previous night's fight and the following restless time in the jail had stirred something in him. Maybe it was a time when he was open to let the past in, like when a man finally opens a window for some air after breathing too much of the room's stink. Whatever it was, the result was that he shuffled some memories from the past like a pack of cards, and the one left on top was his father's face, talking about honour. The fact was that his pa, though a man able to love, was more strongly lured into ruining his own self. The thought that he might do the same, well, that gave Jack Brady a shock of a kind he had never known before.

'Wait! Now young fella . . . I'll be your guard!' He called after Pastor Jim.

By the early afternoon, Sheriff Digby had returned Jack's gun and knife, and watched him walk across to the stable to collect his mare. Pastor Jim was standing in the street waiting for him, with two pack horses.

'Where you goin', Jack?' Sheriff Digby called.

'I'm going to be remembered, Mosey . . . be honourable!'

'Son, what a man needs to think about . . . and we can leave God out of this . . . is how he is seen, now I mean, how he is thought of, now, today.'

The words had even more effect than the pastor's. Jack Brady saw the light. How was he thought of? As a rambling, loose gun, not attached to anything or anybody. Was that how he wanted to be seen? You didn't get a good name by being just another hired man.

The travellers headed out, off to where something significant awaited them, they both knew. Digby watched them and wished them well, saying good luck to himself as he stared.

But the sheriff was not the only observer. Big Evan Wate's stare followed every step Jack took across the windswept summer street, and when Jack and the pastor rode out, slow and steady, they were being trailed by a man with hatred in his heart, and a score to settle.

On the trail to San Antonio, Pastor Jim, who had a natural curiosity about people, had to ask some questions. He knew little about Jack's past, but he knew a lot more about the coming trouble with Mexico than his new friend. When they found a creek they stopped, and the horses went eagerly to the water. The two men sat on rocks. Jack built a cigarette while Pastor Jim watched him, looking into him.

'Jack Brady . . . a good working-man sort of name. That you?'

'Pastor, I have no time for this kind of talk. My mind is fixed on what's ahead.'

'But forgive me, I have to say that it would help if I knew something of your past . . . I'm leading you to join, if they will have you, the Texas Rangers. I'll have to speak for you. They know me and they trust my judgement.'

'Well if you mean fighting, well me and this Appaloosa here, we been together for two years now. My horse, my Paterson revolver, my fists, these are what I can offer the Texans. I know the country. I been working there for some time, after leaving the north. My family were from back east . . . all gone now. The only thing troubling me is the man on my tail. . . .'

'On your tail? What man?'

'Pastor Jim, it could be said that I have a reputation. It's not good. Folk look at me and they think, Jack Brady, the hired gun and the lady's man. See? That's what my life has been. You've stirred somethin' in me . . . suppose you could call it guilt. Some people might look at me and think why do I owe my pa anything . . . he was a failed medical man who liked a drink . . . yet I know he was right about makin' a name, doin' the right thing. I done so many wrong things, that's a fact. Now listen to me, opening up to a God shouter! Never thought I'd see the day. You got some special quality, mister preacher! But you can tell these Texans that I'm useful in a tight spot. I've fought my way out of more than a few of them!'

'And the man coming after you?'

Jack smiled. 'Oh, it's a mistake. Back in some hellish place by the Red River, he says I seduced

16

some woman . . . but I had nothing to do with it . . .
problem is, he's a mental case and I can't reason
with the man.'

'Well I think he'll disappear when we meet up
with Bob Gillespie and his men. I've ridden with
them more than once. Anyway, you'll be too preoc-
cupied to think about a man with a grudge.'

'I hope you're right, Pastor. I sure do. From what
I heard, the Mexicans have one massive army . . . and
we'll be outnumbered.'

'You heard right. But Gillespie's going to like you.
I feel it in my bones.'

'You sure are a young man to be so doggone sure
of Him up there. You had a light from heaven or
somethin'?'

Pastor Jim seemed to find that a tough question,
and he looked down at the dirt, taking some thinking time. Then he looked up, searched the horizon
with his bright, eager eyes, and said, 'I believe that
man's love can be stronger than his hatred. It's a
matter of applying the reason over the animal in us.
A time will come when there will be no war . . . if we
let reason win. For me, I became what I am when I
saw a noble man die for peace, and for reason. He
was my dearest friend, and he gave his life for others
. . . on the trail into Comancheria. He was helping
some travellers who were foolish enough to try to
cross the fringes of that lawless land. He fought to
give the others time to escape. I stayed with him . . .
but I survived. . . .' He lifted his shirt to show a deep

17

red scar across his stomach, and then he raised one hand, to show that two fingers were missing.'

'The *Nemernuh* ... known to most as the Comanches ... they did this. I survived by enduring torture, and I was hanging on to life when the army came and drove my tormentors away. Thing is, God was caring for me ... I believe that, Jack. I knew then that I had a calling in this world.'

Time was that Jack Brady would have laughed at that. But now he kept silent, and went to gather in his horse.

'Maybe that sounded too much like a sermon, Brady ... just let me sum up with the only question that counts in this life: *where are you going*?'

'That's too tough for a straight answer, but meanwhile, let's get to San Antonio, my friend.' He spent a long while running through what he had thought and done over the last few days. It didn't all make sense, but the result was that he had made a decision, and he had to keep to it. Again, something inside nagged at him. Scenes from his past that maybe left some shame, like a footprint that couldn't be shifted, flashed before him as his mind was vacant, his body simply holding the slackened reins as they rode relentlessly south. What had his life been but a series of confrontations? What had he done other than take the dollars and do the job – any job that came his way?

'Mr Brady, you're real quiet. You troubled by something?' Pastor Jim asked.

'Not troubled, just annoyed . . . seems like some flies are bothering me, padre. The invisible kind.'

'Ah, yes. I know them kind of insects. Tend to bite you, tend to make you smart, sore . . . and there's no simple cure.'

'Well, padre, if there are such things as ghosts, and they watch over you, then I'm going to give 'em what they want to see.'

Then they said nothing more, for mile after mile. The heat of the day oppressed them, heavy and close, and they had to ignore the sweat and discomfort. Jack Brady shut the world out: it was something he had learned to be expert at. No more damned jails, and no more pointless fights with the past, which always caught up with you. A man could become bored with the person he had become. He now knew that. But never in his life had he ever considered that a padre would push him to think all these things.

Pastor Jim wasn't sure why Jack was so quiet. It wouldn't do to push him too far. What awaited them in San Antonio was unsure. But then, so was the next minute, and the next hour. What he did not know was that Jack Brady had the problem of the padre's final question running around his mind like a snake that wouldn't let him go, tightening and closing in, tormenting him with those simple words – *where are you going*? He glanced at the padre and thought, well, there's a man who does know where he's going. How do you get hold of that feeling of being sure

19

about something? The only thing he knew for certain is that he saw that this was a question that a man should be able to answer.

2

Some places in the old forgotten borderlands of Texas and Mexico were long-forgotten collections of rotting stables and old saloons, with a few corrals and cheap boarding houses still clinging on to the remains of town life. As time went on, and more of the string of wars and raids from bandits and rebels increased every day, only the more hardy and resilient souls clung on to the roofs over their heads.

What did survive in these places was a room with drink served in a corner and a few forced smiles ready for a man after a long, tiring ride through the oven-hot plains. The men filling these saloons were drifters mostly, lost and aimless types who were satisfied with the dregs of life, as nothing more was an option for them. Such a lost former town was Callego, Mexican in its roots but now calling itself anything as long as it kept visitors happy.

With the war starting to threaten every walk of life, even the usually quiet settlements were nervous.

Anyone could ride in at any time and turn everything upside down, or flatten some homes and ride out again. The men who stayed and fought for the foothold they had worked for were a tough breed; some had handled it until the soldiers started swarming over the borderland, but some few had dug in and gritted their teeth.

The Palace Hotel in Callego had always been a place where men of all kinds could meet and talk, do business and take some time away from their worries. The Guadelupe river was running nearby and folk could spit into Mexican land it was that close. The owner, Bill Cheto, was a mix of so many breeds of man that he could fit in anywhere along the Texas-Mexico border, and he knew almost as many tongues as there were people around the place. He was one of the few who had not been made to run in a panic when war was declared. The Apache in him knew about the wilderness to the north, and the Mexican in him felt that the war, now raging around the place, was more important for Texas than for anyone else.

Consequently, the Texan in him sided with the Rangers who often came by.

He had one stalwart by his side: an orphan called Emilio who had drifted in one day from who knows where, and it was only a matter of hours before Jack Brady arrived in Callego that Bill was wishing his Emilio well, and a safe journey as the young man packed his mustang ready for a special mission.

Emilio, only twenty-five years old and with more energy and spirit than a bronco, was all muscle and rush; there was never enough to do and yet so much to be done in his restless mind. He had been a fiercely loyal Texan since he could walk and say his first words, and now here he was, in McCulloch's Spy Company and set to take a message to Laredo.

'Now, Emilio, keep to the shades, to the dusk . . . move at night. You've checked the pistols, right? Now I want to see you again . . . no risks, right?'

'You fuss and carry on worse than me in one of my moods. I have to deliver this to the Governor at Laredo. That's all I have to worry about. I have food. I have the best horse this side of the Rio Grande . . . I go now!' He mounted up and patted the man he thought of as a father on the shoulder.

Bill slapped the mare's back and said, 'You're all the family I got . . . come back safe!'

Bill Cheto went back to work. He had more than enough to do with the daily chores of running his place, and it was something that couldn't be trusted to anyone else. He had to do every job himself, and had always been like that.

But he also had to cope with some strong individuals, and one of these was making trouble on a night when a group of smart men in suits, with accents placing them well to the north of the Mexican borderlands, were holding a meeting around a table in Cheto's best room. The troublemaker was Bernie Speke, an old-timer with an edge of trouble sharp as a bayonet blade. As Cheto offered his guests more drinks, the row broke out in the saloon – a place usually peaceful, with a few loungers sitting around complaining about the war. Now, with trouble brewing and armies on the move not too far off, the saloon was home to more strangers than usual, and most of them were uneasy, nervous, watching every little movement around them.

Bernie, grey-haired, thin as a rake and armed to the teeth with knives and guns, had been staying there with his daughter while they bought supplies. His place was along the river, half a day's ride away, and he had made it like a fort. It was his own little empire, as he said in conversation. Now, a stranger was rubbing him up the wrong way. Bernie had the man by the collar. 'Who are you to talk of Mexico, mister? You from up north? By your voice I'd say from back East where they chew their words like tough beef. You're talking Mexico in front of a man who has Texas in his heart like a lover. . . .' He threw the man against the bar counter, and matters would have escalated except for a woman's voice from behind old Bernie. 'Pa . . . time for your sleep now. We got to ride home in the morning. I'm real sorry, mister . . . my father likes a drink. . . .' She clutched her father's arm and tugged him away towards the stairs. 'Please forgive him . . . the drink talking!'

The stranger was thinking about reaching for leather and putting a bullet in the old man, but the woman had the manner to soften the hardest heart, and he managed a smile. The other men in the room murmured their approval. 'Now you men . . . see what the power of a good woman can be . . . this is my daughter, Liza. See how she calms me down?'

But there was a man in the corner who was not influenced by the woman's words. He was every inch a gunfighter, and he was known to every man in the room. When he stood up and let his right hand hover over his revolver, the men moved away to the walls, to keep clear. The man was wiry, skin tanned by the sun; he was around thirty and wore a leather vest and leggings as if he had just left off cutting steers out sleeping on the open range.

'Miss, your father insulted my country. Not even your feminine charm will soften my feelings about such a man. I would like you to stand back so your padre and myself may decide who is right and who is wrong.'

'Do as he says, Liza . . . who are you, you Mexican scum?' Bernie challenged.

'You have spoken your last words, old man!'

Bernie pushed Liza away from him, as trouble was coming, but before anything else could happen, the door swung open and Jack Brady came in, followed by Pastor Jim. The new arrivals saw the trouble in a second and reacted. Jack snatched his revolver and the padre spoke by instinct to the men who were facing each other with a murderous passion in their stance.

'Rest easy, gentlemen,' the pastor said, 'I'm a man

of God, and I beg you to stop this hatred, now.'

'I beg you to shut your mouth, holy man. You talk like a monkey . . . no brain and all chattering . . . jabbering like a monkey on a branch. . . .'

Jack moved as quick as a cougar, and he took hold of the Mexican around the midriff, then shoved him to the floor, throwing the weight of his own body on top of him. The man had grasped the gun he had been about to use, and he pulled the trigger as they fell. The bullet hit the doorframe, and made Cheto and others from the meeting rush to the saloon.

There was a considerable crowd around Jack as he took a hold of his prisoner, forcing the man's hand up behind him. He marched him to the door, which Pastor Jim opened, and he threw the man out into the street.

As Jack walked back in, Liza Speke walked towards him. She was auburn-haired and bright-eyed, moving like a cat, he thought. Her look met his eyes, and Jack could think of nothing but her stunning beauty. There was something running through his veins, a rush of feeling he had never known before. 'I have to thank you, from my heart, *señor*. My father . . . he's a hot-head, even with the years he's carrying.' She was tall enough to lean forward and kiss him just standing slightly on her toes, and Jack felt the blush on his skin. The assembled crowd applauded.

As for Bernie Speke, he was sitting on the bottom step of the grand staircase, and inside he was relieved that he hadn't had to face the Mexican. He stood up now, as his daughter walked to be with him again, and he spoke to Jack, 'Mister . . . you're welcome at the Fortress any time you like! I owe you some. . . .'

'Now, time for bed, Pa,' Liza said, and he went with her up the stairs. The men settled back to their talk. But when Jack and Pastor Jim stood at the bar and enjoyed a whiskey, Cheto said, 'Gentlemen, welcome . . . but I have to tell you that the man you threw out was in the Mexican army . . . he works as an agent of some kind . . . I think gun-running. He's part of a *comanchero* outfit. Name's Herrera. We all know they're in the pay of the Mexis, but well, every kind of animal runs along the Guadalupe . . . it's all going to change when the battle comes . . . and it will. See, this war's been brewing for some time. The Mexies . . . they'll call on anybody if it disturbs the States. It's said they even appealed to Britain. Fact is, they were told to pay debts to Americans living in their land and they never did. They challenged the States to a fight and now it's breakin' out like some desert storm that's been simmerin' for some time and then snaps loose. Most folk, they're lookin' for a hole to hide in.'

'What about the old man? What's the Fortress?' Jack asked.

'Oh, that man, well he's my friend, but he sure has some spirit in him! He's a headache around here, but we get on well. I always liked individuals, and he has his own mind about things!' Cheto stopped wiping a wet glass. 'Truth is, he's a general in his head. Sheer imagination! The Fortress is a good ride south, on the river, and he's Bernie Speke. His daughter Liza lives there with him, along with a few desperate men on the run from the law . . . or from themselves, I reckon. Thinks he's leading an army. Hates the Mexicans . . . he told me they wiped out his family home some time back . . . half-crazy I tell you, but maybe I like him because I'm kind of *extreme*, too. One day someone is going to flatten the place and kill them all . . . I fear for young Liza, caught up in all that. But she loves him so much . . . If you're riding that way, you'll see the place . . . looks like an army fort from a distance. You get nearer, you see how rough it all is . . . a matter of planks and barrels. The Rangers have told him to move but he just laughs.'

'That's not where we're heading . . . we're across to the Rangers in San Antonio,' Pastor Jim said.

'Oh, well you're pretty close. They're making ready to join the army I hear. Should be on the move real soon,' Cheto said.

'I'm aimin' to join them,' Jack said, with a broad smile. 'And the pastor here, he's lookin' to take care of their souls!'

'I'm glad you can joke, mister. If they'll have you, then I pray for you both. My son lasted three months. He was my only son. War is good for nobody, my friends. I wish we could all stay out of it . . . like I thought my Palace would until things went out of hand . . . now God only knows who drifts into here . . . the scum of all the South I reckon, and I can tell you one thing for sure . . . as a Ranger, you'll have enemies comin' at you from all sides. The comancheros are a mix of everyone, and they come and go like a dust storm. I wish you luck. A man in the Rangers . . . he don't fight for the money. He don't fight for land. They're like my poor son Abe . . . they go to prove somethin' to themselves.'

Pastor Jim and Jack had been riding slow like, taking their time, since Short Bend, and Jack was aware that his new friend was sounding him out, asking probing questions, wanting to bring out something from the long silence that had been inside Jack Brady. Jack had been seeing more and more clearly, as they had ridden on steadily westwards, that there had been so much wasted time in his life. He was sure that God would never fill the space, but there was a space there, an emptiness. Having time to look at the land somehow backed up that thinking. It was wide, seemingly endless, with bluffs, gullies, arroyos, patches of juniper and mesquite: very little in this part of America invited any human being to stay and put roots down. In a way, that desert landscape made his thoughts even more certain – if the land was against you, then make sure your own self knew some kind of success. That's why the Apaches had been so smart – holing up in their homes in the canyons, feeling safe all dug in and unseen.

Now they were in their cheap single beds in the back rooms of the Palace, and before sleep, the Pastor said, 'Jack Brady, do you make enemies in every place you stop at? First, I find out that a man is after you from way back, and now this Herrera has your name and he wants to put you in a grave. How come you do this?'

'I got a face that provokes folk I guess. Can't change that!' His answer lightened the mood and the pastor turned over in an attempt to find sleep after a long day in the saddle.

However, they lay awake for some time. Jack had so many questions, as the future was uncertain, as always. But this was another new and different life waiting for him in San Antonio. 'Pastor Jim, this war . . . has it started then?'

'The facts are that at the end of last year, Texas became the twenty-eighth state in the United States. Now, Mexico wants to keep Texas Mexican . . . and California. Now it's well into the year of Our Lord, 1846 . . . the volunteers are gathering, to fight for Texas, and yes, the war is on. I heard from one traveller that there's been a battle at Palo Alto, and the Mexies were whipped. But see, they conscript soldiers . . . they got thousands ready to take the place of dead thousands! It's July now, and reports say that the Mexicans are paying all kinds of scum to ride along the borders and set the Indians against Texans as well. Every soul has enemies coming from all sides. . . .'

'Cheerful ain't you? I thought religious types were there to offer comfort.'

'Comfort, yes. Lies, no, my friend! Now sleep.'

But sleep paid no visit to Jack Brady that night. He and Pastor Jim had been riding through the heat, wrapped around by a desert storm at one time, and they had taken cover in an arroyo. There had been time to think, and he had said to himself, as he took a drop of water and wiped the sweat from his brow, that he was going to make that name and be remembered. But now, with Cheto's words in his head – *provin' somethin' to themselves* – he knew the hotel owner was right. But there was something more a man needed. He was beginning to see that. What he needed was in the woman who had met his look and kissed his cheek. Yes, Liza Speke had opened up some kind of need. It was a need he didn't know was there until that night. He had known the embrace of a woman, but that had been something without feeling, like satisfying the thirst of a parched steer at a stream.

Where are you going? he thought yet again. A woman had given some kind of answer to that. Jack found himself tussling with a line of thought he had never known before: *life was not always necessarily a one-man ride from nowhere to nowhere.*

3

'Ladies and gentlemen, good townsfolk and strangers passing through, I'm asking for a few minutes of your time. . . .' The speaker was standing high, on a little stage made of wooden boxes, placed slightly dangerously on a walk board by the side of the main street of San Antonio, and as Pastor Jim and Jack Brady rode into the place, they caught the eye of the man addressing the crowd. He was dignified, scholarly, and dressed in sober black. People did stop to listen. He seemed well respected. He had his hands in his vest pockets and swayed from side to side, taking out an arm from time to time to drive a point home.

'Why can't you speak straight and plain, mister?' a voice asked from the crowd.

'I am speaking honest . . . and my paper tells you the facts, the truth. . . .'

'You should pick up a gun, not write them fancy words!' There was laughter running through the crowd. But the speaker was unmoved and did not react.

'Ladies, gentlemen, all you good people . . . I have no intention to cause a panic, but I merely warn you all of what is to come. The war is upon us, and war is a ghastly thing to contemplate. I am Walt Buchanan, teacher once in this town . . . now a man driving hard into politics with my *Texas Debater* periodical . . . which is for sale here today . . . now I stand here to remind you of this noble community which has known the terror of violent death and sacrifice for too long now . . . the mission of San Antonio de Valero was the scene of a desperate battle only ten years back . . . the ghosts of the dead walk the streets, begging for men to volunteer and take on the Mexican oppressor. I'm speaking for that now. This town is growing. It still has hope. On the south bank we have German folk . . . Europeans come here, to La Villita . . . this community must survive. I ask you to gather your weapons and fight. . . .'

He paused and then addressed Jack and Pastor Jim. 'You are new arrivals, gentlemen . . . may I ask, are you here to fight for freedom?'

'For Texas and for an end to despotism! But with God on our side!' Pastor Jim replied, and the crowd, who had turned to look at the strangers, cheered.

'Fine, fine. Now, as it happens I have with me a man who works as my correspondent along the border, and he has something to say . . . tell the good people what's happening, Barney.'

A man with the build of a wrestler stood up on the makeshift stage, wiping dirt from his face. 'I've just come from watching the enemy we really have to fear . . . the *comancheros* are rousting up any natives who bear a grudge . . . there's silver passing from hand to palm and there's our own fiend, Herrera, he's the man we have to rub out. Read my report in the Debater.' He held up a copy of the paper and waved it in the breeze.

The speakers stopped and shouted out the name of the newspaper. The crowd dispersed. Pastor Jim and Jack left their mounts in the stables and paid the ostlers there well. It was time to contact the fighting men.

The town was rippling with activity. There were riders, wagons, walkers and noise on every thoroughfare. The signs of war were everywhere: ruined walls, holes in buildings, heaps of rubble and broken furniture on every corner. There were waifs wandering the streets and all kinds of underfed, partly clothed drifters were brushing past gentlemen in suits and ladies in finery. There was a stink of flesh in the air, too. Jack Brady knew that smell from his time on the cattle trails.

Pastor Jim knew where he was heading. They were soon standing outside an old Hispanic part-ruin with a balcony, on which three armed men stood ready and shouted down, asking the names of the visitors, but then another man joined them and laughed, calling down, 'Pastor . . . you're still alive and kicking! Come on in.'

Inside, sitting at a long table covered in papers and glasses, was the man who had called down. Pastor Jim walked in ahead of Jack, held out a hand, and as the man stood up and shook his hands, the Pastor said, 'Robert Gillespie . . . good to see you again. Robert, this is Jack Brady, and he wants to volunteer.'

Gillespie, wearing a dark jacket and white trousers, was thick set, with rich black hair. He moved stiffly as he walked around the table and shook hands with Jack Brady. They met eye-to-eye, and they were both young men. For a leader, Gillespie was hardly a grey-haired old scrapper. He was in his thirties, bluff, direct and of few words.

'You're here to be a Volunteer, Brady? You got your own Paterson Colt I see . . . horse?'

'Appaloosa . . . strong mare. Been with me for three years. I broke her in. She's maybe around six.'

'You know what you're volunteering for?' Jack shook his head, and Gillespie motioned for them to sit down. He poured some coffee. 'Cold now, I fear, but you'll be living on this . . . food is supplied. Everything else you bring. You'll have all basic provisions I trust?'

Jack smiled, took a swig of coffee and pulled a face. 'Ah, yes . . . thick as mud! But I got everything you'd expect a cowpuncher to have. Money doesn't figure. I heard about Texas being outnumbered, and I'm here to join the line.'

35

'Fine. What we can do is give you a second revolver . . . you'll need two reliable ones, the way we fight.' He saw that his listener was not entirely understanding the point. Jack said simply, 'Well I can learn to fight any way you want, mister.'

Gillespie's face was severe now. He was feeling the pain from a wound, and Pastor Jim explained. 'Jack, Bob Gillespie here was at Palo Alto . . . took a blade!'

'Palo Alto! I heard about that.'

'It was mostly about the cannon. We came out well. Now, Mister Brady, I have to give you some hard facts. See, the situation is that Mexico, they want the border at the Nueces. We want it a good way south at the Rio Grande. The armies are regrouping after two actions, and the enemy are using all kinds of outfits in their pay to harass the borderlands. Where we need men like you is against these pockets of Mexies and other roving scum . . . they're even bringing in Indians and *comanchero* bands . . . if we can use patrols to stifle this, then the coming battles will be evened out some . . . you see?'

Jack nodded. He could patrol all right. He could move by night and hit hard where he had to.

'Mister Brady, if you can ride, shoot and most of all, take orders, then you can ride with me and my patrol. We leave in three days. You sign up for six months, agreed? You look hale and hearty. You have a look of a man who's known considerable rough play . . . fists and guns. Right?'

'Yep, I see my fair share of that.'

'You say you're fighting for Texas. You a *tejano*?'

'No. Born back east. Pa was a doctor. I learned some of that trade from him . . . but I went wandering and learned how to survive . . . where to squeeze out water when parched and how to treat a bite from any damned critter out past civilized life.'

'Well you're about to meet plenty of those critters, mister. Welcome to the war. There's going to be a regiment of Texan riflemen, but until then, we're a rowdy mix of troublemakers, out to stop General Arista and his partners from running over our land. Many have died for that land, Brady. Report back here first light in three days' time. Bring some salt, hardtack, a blanket . . . you have a good knife?'

Jack nodded.

'Good. You will be sleeping fully clothed and under the moon. If you've ridden and pushed cattle you'll know all about doing without most of life's little comforts. Still want to join up?'

Jack nodded again and added, 'Got somethin' to do, Sir, and your war seems to be just the place to do it.' He saluted and met a salute in return.

'Mr Brady . . . you'll see dragoons . . . all in sweet, fresh blue, with officers fresh from West Point. You'll sometimes fight alongside these men. They think they are the *real* soldiers. You savvy?'

'Yep. I met some. Patience needed. I won't start any trouble with 'em.'

'You're reading my mind . . . dismissed!'

*

Some hours later, as Pastor Jim caught up with some sleep, Jack went out to shift his thirst and clear the desert dust out of his throat. There was no shortage of cantinas and little ramshackle hotels and bars. Every street corner had its restless crowd, and people were shouting and singing in the dirt-thick streets. One drinking hole looked as good as another, but somehow he felt the need to mix with Texans, and he asked a sober-looking man with an official-seeming appearance where there was a drink and a chair to be had among Texan Volunteers. He could meet some of his future fellow fighters.

A bar was pointed out, the Cantina Donoho, and as he walked inside, the level of sound from around fifty men who stumbled round shrieking and hollering, and grabbing each other in a rough but friendly way, he noticed a space in the bar and made for it, snapping out an order for a whiskey from the old barman. As the drink was handed over, the little, rotund man asked why he was in San Antonio, but before Jack could answer there was a tap on his shoulder and he turned to see the familiar face of Evan Wate. Jack had to look up, as before, to look into the man's eyes. They were cold as ever.

'Ah, Jack Brady, again. This time, I'm callin' you out!' He snapped this out with such force that the bar was silenced and space was made behind Wate, who stepped back several paces and stood with his hands held still, above the revolvers on each side of his waist. The holsters were strung low, and Wate wore only a vest, with no coat.

'First time I saw you, Wate, you were wearing a slicker and the rain was drenching us both. It was the day that your sister met Square John Duro. He's the man you want. I never harmed your sister!'

'Now boys . . . save your bullets for the Mexicans!' This was the voice of the barman, but he spoke in vain.

'I'm tired of trackin' you across this damned oven of a country . . . and I been dodgin' Comanches and all kinds of brigands out there. Now's the time to settle it. I ain't goin' home without the thought that I put you under the dirt for a real long time, Brady!'

More bystanders shuffled around behind Wate, and tables were left clear. Bullets would only slam into the window or the door. Jack Brady had been in that situation so many times, he knew the best way to work things. His right hand was hovering over leather, and his Paterson Colt was always reliable. The years had given him the confidence that tough survival brings. When Wate went for his guns, in a split-second, Jack moved sideways, and as he moved, he brought up his gun and shot in one swift movement. The bullet cracked into Wate's left arm, as the tall man's own slugs went wide of their mark.

'Now, is it over, Wate? Are we done?' Jack asked, standing over the man.

Wate grimaced and held his arm. Blood seeped out across his fingers. A rush of men went to him and someone shouted for a doctor.

'Don't bother . . . get him in the back room . . . bring hot water and a clean cloth. I'll need scissors. . . .' Jack called out.

Wate was carried to a table in a small room at the back of the cantina. But when he saw that Jack was about to treat him he snarled, 'He can't touch me . . . the scum! Get me a real doc, right?' The crowd listened and, quietly, Jack was asked to leave. As he walked out into the hot night, Wate's voice screamed behind him, 'This ain't over, Jack Brady . . . I'm comin' for you.'

In the moonlight, striding slowly back to his hotel, Jack took in the skyline of cracked wood and adobe; strong smells of meat cooking filled the air. There was laughter. He knew, as he had met this so many times before, that all this gaiety was what people did when death was just a short way down the trail, and no futures were guaranteed. As he looked around, he saw a newspaper being blown on the wind, down past his feet. He picked it up and read the headline: 'Trouble along the Grande . . . Koni Herrera's men let hell loose. . . .' He read the first paragraph, and there he had an account of a familiar character:

Koni Herrera, half-breed Mexican fighter, along with his rag-tag army of mercenaries, has been seen moving along the Rio Grande, and looking for trouble. He is the first line of the Mexican army, whose strategy is to instil fear on all Texan communities along the river. The editor fears for the lives of several of this paper's old friends, including local patriot Bernard Speke and his family at the Fortress. . . .

Koni Herrera: the man he had met at The Palace. So he was in the fight, too. Jack Brady had three days to act. He had to get out to the Fortress and back again in three days. That's what the voice inside told him to do. But he was just one man. Herrera had a small army. There was one more option: he had to talk Gillespie into taking his patrol out without delay. Maybe the padre would speak for him. But how could a raw recruit sway a commanding officer? Again, impossible.

One option was left: he would ride out, down the river, and scout, see if anything could be done. It was in the hands of fate. If it came to a choice between being a recruit and standing by the side of Speke, who was remaining firm in the face of the engulfing tide of war, then Jack would choose the quickest way to join a scrap. Even more in his mind was the thought that Liza was there, most likely in a heap of trouble, and in need of urgent help. It was the same as a thousand decisions he had taken in his life long before that day in Texas: rash, ill-thought out and most likely dangerous. But then, when had life ever been all sweetness and laughter? It all came down to a plain decision – war or woman? She needed him far more than Gillespie.

4

Pastor Jim was at the bedside of the man who had sent for him. This was Bullhead Peters, a Ranger who had stopped a bullet and felt the slash of a knife more than once in his fighting life. He had joined up ten years back, when the notion of a Ranger force was very new, and hardly anyone knew about them at all. They had then fought almost exclusively against various Indian groups, especially the war parties venturing south from Comancheria. When the Comanches took it into their head to have a little jaunt down the plain and terrify settlers it was like a pleasant meadow turning into hell, and the few Rangers in Texas had tried to stop at least some of these attacks.

Bullhead had been arguably the best close fighter of the Texans on their trips out to face the wild men of the plains. He had survived for a long time, but now, he was confined to his bed, and everyone around him knew that his days were short.

'Jim, good to see you, young buck. I think he's caught up with me at last . . . the Dark Hunter. He's been on my tail more n' once. But the doc says this time my lungs is givin' out. He says too much smokin' and drinkin'. I always wanted to die in a fight, but I'm bein' denied that, my friend!' He was a broad, strong man, big-backed, stacked with muscle, and hence his name. All the Rangers had special names, mostly as compliments. Bullhead was a bar-room fighter, one who raged like a crazed cougar.

'Jim . . . I like to think that I'm the closest thing to a pa you ever had. That right?'

'That's right. You taught me all I know, except for the Comanche . . . they taught me something else. Something you can't buy anywhere in this world. It's strange, Bill, but the pagans taught me more than the Christians!'

'Yeah, I read you right, young man . . . I've hated 'em and slaughtered 'em, but I've respected the savages as well. The one thing I can't forgive, in all my years agin 'em, is the way they treat women. They have no heart . . . at least, not where folks like us is concerned.'

Bullhead turned in his bed, trying to get more comfortable, and in doing this he coughed. A woman nursing him came rushing to him with a cup of water and tried to help him drink. 'Bill . . . try to drink some, please!' He tried, then almost choked, and coughed until he was red raw. The nurse waited for this to pass and then went away.

'See what a state I'm in? I might as well just hand in my deck and leave the damned game, right? Now Jim, I called you for a reason. I want to say goodbye, sure. But I want you to do somethin' for me. See, my little partner, Emilio ... he's all I got ... I lost my wife to some murderin' bandits when we was on the Pecos river. He's at Bill Cheto's, and Bill took him in like a son. He was all alone after some kind of massacre ... but I took him under my wing when he joined up. He's like a son to me, and Bill knows it. We let him take my name, so he's a Peters! Stuck with my unlucky name, poor kid! Well, he's one of the fighters for Texas and he's on a special mission ... now, he's asked a girl to marry him. She took his ring. Now, if you could just see she's all right? Could you look in on her if you're down Laredo way?'

'Well sure, if I can find her. Who is she?'

'You know a place run by Bernard Speke? On the Grande? She's his daughter, Liza.'

'I've seen her. I'll try, old friend. I'll try. Problem is, I'm riding with the Volunteers, as a padre.' He knew nothing of Jack Brady's feelings about the girl.

'Well, find a way, will you? Just find a way to keep her safe. That boy Emilio loves her. I think she loves him. They're to marry when everything stops makin' the world dizzy! Anyway, he's a Ranger. . . . He's with Gillespie's men. Turnin' the new boys into fighters!' His breathing became noisy and he fought for breath again. The nurse came and she asked Pastor

Jim to leave. 'We might need you soon,' she whispered, 'in your professional role, I mean.'

He kissed Bullhead's forehead and said, softly, 'Bill, try to sleep . . . try to sleep, Pa!'

The old man smiled.

Emilio Peters was aware that for the first time, he had the tormenting feeling that he was lost. The land had been familiar so far, as he rode at a moderate pace in the direction of what he thought was the south and the Rio Grande, but by nightfall he sensed that he was a little off track, and there was nothing for it but to bed down for a while and sleep, then look for one of the many landmarks he had in his head from years of riding that stretch of Texan territory. Old Bullhead had made a fighter of him, teaching him how to survive in the desert and how to use any weapon that came into his hands. Yes, he felt as though two fathers worried about him, and they both taught him well. His fellow Rangers teased him for having the 'two Bills' rubbing his hair and lecturing him on how to throw a knife and how to break a bronco.

Just as dawn turned the horizon amber, he was riding again, slow and easy, and he saw in the distance the unmistakeable canyon of Abuelo. If he rode south of that, he would be heading for the river. On he went, with his eyes scanning the distance on all sides, checking for the smallest movement. If a prairie dog cocked a leg, he would

45

sense it. The great canyon came closer and closer, until he was within a few hundred yards, but then he heard noise and pulled up. He managed to hide himself and horse in a patch of curl-leaf shrubs and some rocks; there was the sound of men and horses – so loud as to be unnerving to his mare.

Emilio decided to creep cautiously closer, but no sooner had he moved a limb than a line of riders came out of the canyon. There were hundreds of them. The line went on and on. By the time they were out and there was an empty space behind them, he reckoned there were around four hundred men there. They were Mexican military, and mixed in were some Apaches and other Indians he didn't recognize.

Where could they be going? They were moving south, that was for sure. If only he could tell Ben McCulloch . . . but all he could do was resolve to follow them, at a careful distance. Chances were, he thought, that they were on their way to some major engagement, but what were they doing so far north?

They had scouts. The Apaches would be circling the line. He could be seen. In fact, they could be close to him now. Bright day was filling the air and making the world open to all inspection, from vultures up high to rattlers in the dust. All he could do was crawl, step as easy as a man on broken glass, and pray that he had not been seen.

*

Jack Brady could think of nothing but Liza and the Fortress as he stood in a line of around a dozen men who were listening to Gillespie. Jack, looking around, saw faces betraying very much his own feelings: a mix of apprehension and excitement. The recruits were of all shapes, sizes, colours and dispositions. There were sun-tanned prairie men, well-fed suited types, some blacks and some whites, and one or two whose kin could have been hard to define. But they had one thing in common: they wanted to defend Texas and the United States.

'Now, I've spoken to you all . . . or Mr McCulloch has . . . and you are accepted men. Accepted . . . and almost trained . . . except for the new men! But another few days, and training will be complete. You men will see some action very soon . . . I know you're itching to fight, but be patient just a mite longer. Some have been turned away. You're the best. Every volunteer was spillin' over with enthusiasm, but we ask more than that. You have all brought mounts, guns and knives. The good news is that we have some weapons now, to hand over to you if you're short. Two revolvers and a rifle are absolutely essential to the way we fight. As for food . . . I hope you all have the rations we asked for, all packed up and ready. Where you'll be goin' there may be no food ready. We have to kill our dinner as we move along. Now, very soon, we're headin' out to Laredo. This is on the border. You will see plenty of the enemy, strung out in gangs, all doin' their feelin' out for our

47

strength and our movements. All clear so far? Any questions?'

A man in black, suggesting more an undertaker than a fighter, kicked some dirt, looked all moody, and then looked up at the officer. 'Sir, we all six-month men?'

'Yes, you all signed for six months. I have to be frank with you all. What you are doing is extremely dangerous. We are to spy, skirmish, meet with rangin' groups of the enemy, men doin' the same as we are. We could face death at any time. The odds on all of you coming back to San Antonio are pretty slim.' He stopped and looked around. The men took in that hard fact, some with a wry smile and some with a nervous glance at their new comrades.

'Now, by the way, I will be leading you. You will address me as Captain Gillespie. I am to join a larger force under General Taylor, and you will then be ready to meet an army in battle. Not all of you will be with me then. Who knows how long our work will take around Laredo. But there is one thing for sure – we are outnumbered.'

He looked around for a while, expecting comments, but none came.

'The Volunteers are not a regular army, of course, but officers expect some kind of discipline. Follow orders and all will be well. We make for the Rio Grande pretty soon. We have a few days to get you sharpened up like we want you to . . . normally takes months, but we got a week! Get some rest . . . eat well

. . . be ready to sleep under the night sky. You are putting your lives at risk for Texas and for the United States, who have not accepted terms from Mexico . . . we also still feel the hurt of what happened at the mission here a decade ago, when men died facing impossible odds. This is the moment for us to hit back – do not forget that we have to have two revolvers and a rifle. I have to keep reminding you of the fact. It's the fact that helps keep a man alive in this outfit . . . you got that? That's because we fight at the charge. We ride hard and hit 'em hard . . . even Comanches! We need to have you sharpened up and learn you the ways of Hays, as we call it.'

'Sir . . . Captain Gillespie, Sir . . . we going to see Hays?' a voice asked from the line.

'Ah, yes. Now in case anyone here is not aware of the fact, our commander is John Coffee Hays.' There were murmurs in the line as men gave their responses, and all these were expressing admiration.

'Yes,' Gillespie went on, 'Colonel Jack Hays is our commanding officer. You may see him at times, but mostly he'll be way ahead. Remember, we're sweepin' up the marauders, the rough-riders out to harass us and make some panic happen. Colonel Hays is feared and respected across the whole of Texas and beyond . . . the Comanches call him Capitan Yack. Should you meet him, you salute and call him Sir, right? Now dismiss!'

Pastor Jim had not joined the line-up. He was considered to be non-combatant. Jack wondered how a padre could survive in the tracks of death they were about to take. *There's no armour in a prayer*, his pa had always said, and that stuck.

But there was a week before they set out. Jack took in that hard fact and thought about Liza Speke. Her father needed help now, it seemed. There was no time to lose. He would have to get permission to delay his training. There was nothing for it but to head out now, down south to the Grande. His only chance was for Pastor Jim to spin a yarn.

'Padre . . . you have to tell Gillespie that I'm sick. I need a week. Can you do that? There's somewhere I have to be. It's best I don't tell you, as I know you would tag along. This is for me to do . . . no sense risking your neck!'

'Just make sure you come back, Jack Brady. There's no need for me to tell lies . . . I'll tell him the truth. Just take care.'

'I'll do my best!'

'What I can do, if the route you're taking is towards Laredo, is try to persuade the colonel that your mission is an honourable one, and against Herrera. My friend Bullhead will surely speak for us. Are you heading south?'

'Tell the Colonel I am . . . that will help.'

The pastor listened and thought about trying to say anything else that might change his mind, but he knew the man by now. Before dawn, Jack Brady was heading out for the Fortress, and nobody knew. There would be no help if things went wrong.

*

That night, Pastor Jim had his wish. He sat with Bullhead and explained the situation. The man was well enough to talk, though quietly, and his words were packed with experience. 'You say your young friend is heading south . . . alone? Well God help him. Unless he knows how to stay invisible and move in the dark mainly, he'll be seen by every pair of eyes, animal and human, over the hundred miles or so.'

'But I need to persuade Gillespie not to reject Jack . . . technically he's already disobeying orders . . . signing on and then being away, like a free citizen.'

Bullhead managed a wry smile. 'Rules is made to be broken. Hays and Gillespie put more store on a man's ability. I'll get a message to Jack Hays . . . let's go right to the top!'

The night closed in, and a coolness gave some respite to the men now sitting around in San Antonio, who knew something of what lay ahead when they became fighters for the Lone Star state, so new and fresh like a yearling. But, like a young creature, Texas had the ordeal of a struggle for life, and the first task was to rid its plains of the vermin infesting it.

Jack Brady, though born in the east, had tasted the worst that the plains and deserts of the south and west could inflict on a man, went on his quest, and all he could see in his mind was the face of Liza.

51

5

Jack made his preparations. A study of the maps made it clear that all the activity he knew about was between San Antonio and Laredo. The Volunteers and their Ranger leaders would soon be travelling that way. If the war carried on tightening up, then the main stretch of road down to Monterrey would be the quickest route for whatever force was on the move. But word had it that Herrera and bands of fighters like his were out to scout, to do reconnaissance and to harass Texans and settlers at every opportunity.

Surely, so his thinking went, the tracks through the borderlands would be well used and easily seen, and so scouting would not be so tough. It was the kind of land where any blur of movement was seen and noted. Any creature or human crawling around like a shadow would likely survive.

Jack, with horse and weapons ready, along with basic food and a blanket, paused in the stables to read again the paper cutting he kept in his pocket, wrapped in a fold of string card: it was a piece about his father, in the time before it all went wrong with drink. He sat and uncreased the paper, and there it was again, that heading: *Medical Man saves Governor.*

There it was in print – proof that his father had done something remarkable. He *had* made a mark. There was the important statement: '*Dr Brady told our reporter that Governor Tate had suffered a seizure while at the Masonic Dinner, taking place for raising funds for orphans. . . .*' His father had acted swiftly and saved a life. He had kept a human heart beating and sent a man back to his wife and family who could easily have left this life.

With a smile and some thoughts murmured to himself, Jack put the cutting away again in his pocket and swung into the saddle. His mind was in turmoil, thinking of the Mexicans rampaging across the open land and the bare desert between San Antonio and the sea, and across the south of Texas. Yes, he was there to help keep that land free, but in his mind the lovely face of Liza Speke was always there. He could not explain to others, if asked, what was happening to him; even more difficult was the job of explaining to himself why he couldn't keep her from his thoughts.

As he rode slowly out into the cool air, he was wrapped up in thoughts about her. He dared to allow the fanciful line of thought that here might be destined for him that creature he never knew nor understood, the wife. If he ever had a wife, it would be Liza. Then, even thinking of the word made him shake himself into reality again. Jack Brady, he said to himself, *you're letting the plain facts of hard life run like water, away from you. Pull yourself together, man.*

But as he pushed his mare to a little more pace, he felt a shiver of mixed joy and fear at what he had been daring to consider.

Jack Brady had known the loneliness of the plains and the desert. The endless open spaces of the borderlands and the stretches of Indian land further north and east held no terrors for him. His life had taught him that life could be sustained on very little. He and his Appaloosa mare knew each other well, and though food might be short and water never sure, both horse and man knew deep down that the worst enemy out in the vastness before him now was in a man's mind – the fear he imagined. Every scrap of trouble that had ever come his way was something he could handle alone. But now, so many others depended on him. That was more disturbing than any Mexican or rebel bandit.

He had become accustomed to seeing movement in the distance, and his look roved across the emptiness, looking for the slightest change of colour or flicker of action. Only a fool would assume that nobody watched him. He knew they did, of course. But the first day went well. He sensed no danger, and when dusk came, he found a spot in a dried out arroyo with a small creek and some shade from cottonwood trees. No fire was possible, so he tethered the mare, put the saddle down as a pillow and ate some hardtack and some sugar from his wallet. As he ate, he looked around furtively, taking in every sound. Some noises he knew well, such as that of a snake or a lizard; others were unfamiliar. There was a firm breeze and so the vegetation was stirred.

His mind tormented him with thoughts about Liza and her father. Could they be safe? The old man was surely overconfident, planted in ground out there where every military movement would be along the river. His enemies were not clear either. But one thing was clear in Jack's mind – he was going for Liza. It was for her that he was going alone through such dangerous territory. He brought to mind the look they gave each other in the hotel. Though never spoken, there was something understood that time. He felt that she had recognized his strong feelings for her. Never before had he met a woman who stirred him so, and affected him so deeply. Now here he was, going to do what he thought to be a rescue mission, as he imagined her under attack at the place where her father had dug in and made his own fragile destiny. He was probably caught between the parties in the developing war, and he might well be everybody's enemy. Or he might just be in the way of an army on the move. The thoughts would not let him sleep.

As it turned out, this was good. The reason being

that in the middle of the night, with the moon above shrouded in cloud, Jack sensed something moving, and it was human. He tensed every muscle in his body and kept rigidly still, listening intently as another rustle was heard, now much closer.

Jack cocked his revolver and slid off his hat so he could see around better, but in that few seconds there was a sudden weight on him, and a fist slammed into his jaw. Someone had him by the neck and was pushing him into the dirt. In the dark, all he could make out was a face with a beard, but there was no time to think. Instinct kicked in and Jack let fly a punch to the attacker's chin. The man reeled back, shouting, 'Jack Brady . . . it only takes one hand to handle a gun. . . .'

The figure stood up, firing a bullet at Jack, which whistled past an ear and shattered some rock. It was Evan Wate, again. One arm was bandaged, after their last encounter. Now, before the tall man could move again, Jack was on him and had him in a tight hold, pressed to an earth bank behind.

'Evan Wate . . . listen real good. I did not offend any women of your blood or acquaintance. Leave off this madness, I beg of you. Enough is enough.' He took the man's gun and stepped back, releasing his captive, who staggered back and then sat down in the dust. Jack put his own gun away and put Wate's pistol out of reach, behind the saddle.

'I been told different, Brady. You can prove what you say?'

'I could if we were back home, 400 miles away! You have to believe me . . . the men you spoke to mistook me for a man called Square John, like I told you . . . it's happened before. We were on a drive together . . . once in some little dirt town close to Wichita the same thing happened . . . John is a ladies' man and he sure looks like my kid brother. I'm telling the truth.'

Evan Wate looked long and hard at the man he had pursued across hundreds of miles of waste land. He spat some blood from his mouth and then felt the sore lump on his face. 'Well, fact is, I was gettin' bored anyways. I guess I'll have to believe you, mister. I reckon you're unkillable, if that's a word . . . I mean, you're tougher than old beef and more wily than a sidewinder in a shadow. What are we gonna do now?'

'Well, I can't trust a man who's trailed me all that way. Such a man must have a hurt deep inside that you can't just wipe out in a minute. Trust comes dear in this situation, my friend!'

Wate managed a smile and then wiped some blood from his nose. 'You know, I'd rather be with you than agin' you, Brady. I can't totally believe you, but seems like we both. . . .'

He was cut short. They both heard sounds of movement, and too close for comfort. Jack nodded towards the cottonwoods and they both scampered for cover into what patches of green and yellow they could find, where they squat and watched.

57

Two men walked into the little clearing, bowed down as if trying to keep small and safe.

Scarcely had Jack yelled out a cry to strike some fear into them, and sprung out to confront the men, than another man jumped Evan Wate from behind. If Wate still had some frustrated wrath in him, it now had a target. The man who sprang on him was small and thin. The big man took the man's leg and swung him around, then flung him out into the clearing. As this happened, Jack had struck hard with his fist at the nearest man and then darted for his saddle to grab his rifle. He was thumped behind by something hard and took the blow, then swung his rifle behind, where it smashed into the second man's face and knocked him out. The other assailant was staggering to his feet, and as he did so, Evan Wate's long arm – the only one he could use – swung into him, the fist cracking him square on the jaw.

The three attackers now lay on the ground, one of them unconscious. Jack's Paterson now pointed at them, and Wate's one free hand held a knife.

'Who are you? What do you want?' Evan asked, threat in his voice.

They were young, Mexican. The man laid out flat was white. 'Señor . . . do not shoot, I beg!' The man with the gun to his head said.

Jack tried a guess and it hit home. 'Herrera . . . you with him?'

The man nodded. '*Sí* . . . Herrera . . . many more behind us!'

'Tie 'em up . . . tie 'em with the other,' Wate said. Jack made himself busy with that, while Wate kept a barrel pointing at them.

The Mexicans were hog-tied, hands and feet, and left, as Jack and Wate rode out of there fast. After an hour's hard riding towards the Grande, Wate said, 'Brady, could you use a partner?'

'Well, for a big man, you move real sharp . . . you'll do! I could use another gun.'

'Just one thing I think would be useful to know, Brady . . . where are we goin' – I mean to hell or heaven?' Wate asked.

'Oh . . . to the Rio Grande, to help some folks in a bad way.'

'Some folks?'

'Well, in particular, a woman.'

'A woman?' As he asked this, Evan Wate could not resist the humour of the situation. 'You sure I can trust you, Brady? I mean here we are, not fightin' for the time bein' . . . and seems you're mixed up with a woman again. What a surprise . . . I think you're spinnin' me a line, Brady. But for now, until you prove yourself, I'll ride with you. This place we're goin' . . . is it likely to be dangerous?'

'Sure is. From what I hear, it's best described as a bunch of diehard Texans keeping an army at bay. That sound inviting, Mister Wate?'

'Yep . . . but remember I only have one arm available. Some maniac on the loose shot me, back there, in a two-bit border town.'

'Name of Jack Brady?'

'How did you know that? See, he's so dangerous, he's known everywhere. . . .' He was enjoying the joke. Maybe the angry man was still inside him somewhere, but the two now shared a common enemy, and that brings enemies together and sometimes cools the temper, or maybe even changes opinions.

Jack Brady never said it, but inside he was thinking that maybe, just sometimes, the men who hate you can make the best partners.

The Fortress was exactly that, but not the orthodox thing that a military thinker might have called it if he inspected it. On the bank of the Rio Grande, thirty miles west of Laredo, Bernie Speke had put down roots. The home he defended was a row of adobe homes and two stabling blocks, with rough stone and wood-board parapets along the desert side, and the river behind, where his three boats were moored, one of them a row-boat long and broad enough to take thirty men on board, but with an old hut for a cabin. That would give shelter to maybe half a dozen people, but anyone else would be open to the weather. The other craft were hardly to be trusted, one being an old half-wrecked steamboat that was used before the Brazos took over as the river for the bigger boats. Speke had made the place a refuge for anyone running from trouble or in need of food and shelter. In his own mind he thought of the Fortress as a small town.

Bernie Speke and his daughter had made a pact, after losing their family to a *comanchero* band north of the Nueces, that they would be strong, be tough enough to never, ever again be victims. More than that, they swore to gather and protect anyone looking for a home if they seemed to be on the right side of clean morals.

The place had become one of the best corners of the borderlands to find shelter and protection. Every drifter, every hunted bandit and every lost soul seemed to be washed up there, at least in Speke's eyes. But one thing they all faced now: the threat from Mexico, who now wanted to keep Texas and many another territory, from California across to the east.

July was full of heat and dust as Speke looked out and waited for the horizon to be lined with horsemen. He had no cannon. If he faced cavalry, then he could fight with an advantage, and the same for infantry. But if Mexican conscripts turned up with cannon, then his fort would soon yield. On that July day, he watched and waited, and prayed also, in between the conversations with his trusted friends. But there was another problem: the sick.

Liza came to him on the parapet and she looked more worried than usual.

'Pa, we had two more come in last night . . . survived an attack and ran from their village. We now have twenty sick. We're not a hospital. We have no doctor. But we can't turn them away. What shall I do?'

'Daughter, you can only keep them warm, fed and safe. After that, we pray they can sleep, if pain will let them. Sometimes the worst wounds are the unseen ones. Give them comforting words . . . I know you will . . . and coffee.'

'Pa, we do that. It helps, but we are going to lose some . . . some have fevers . . . we need medicine . . . but look!' Her voice changed from matter-of-fact to shock, and she pointed out across the plain. There was dust and there were men on horses, lots of them.

6

The same band of horsemen were seen by Jack Brady and Evan Wate, who were riding steadily around a mile to the north, and they stopped while Wate took out his eyeglass. 'Mexies . . . maybe army . . . others mixed with 'em though. Must be close to Speke.'

'My money says it's Herrera. We have to help them . . . come on, we'll ride through 'em!'

'Ride through 'em? No we will not. I'm not ready to die today, Brady. This is a war. There could be hundreds of Mexies out there. Listen . . . we get closer, and we do our best to see exactly what's happening . . . we need facts.'

This was not the Brady way, but Jack saw the sense in the argument and he nodded. 'Fine. Let's move slow, find a position with some height . . . have a look-see. But if the Fortress is in trouble, I'll have to go in!'

By late afternoon they had wound well clear of the

Mexican band, aware that the horses would churn up dirt. There was a canyon mouth around a mile to the north and they climbed that, easy and slow, before squatting at around 100 feet up, and from there they could see the Fortress. The glasses gave them a good view. Jack looked and combed the ranks of the assailants, finding Herrera himself, sitting by a makeshift stretch of canvas over some rocks and stakes. He had three other men with him, close up, and then beyond, there was a force of maybe a hundred men, all around their horses, sitting, eating and looking restless. Light would soon be fading. Were they going to attack soon?

Wate thought they would – any minute now.

'No, wait . . . the horses are being rounded up . . . the men are making camp. We have some time,' Jack said, still looking through the glasses. 'They'll make fires . . . there's nobody they fear.'

What they could not see, because it was five miles further east, was the battalion of Mexicans arching around to meet Herrera's force, after pausing by the riverbank on the Gulf side. They were still being tailed by Emilio Peters, whose luck was holding out, but he had seen that the Mexicans were closing on the river, and he knew that the Fortress was nearby. Everything pointed to the Spekes being crushed, completely outnumbered.

He could only watch and wait, but the one thing open to him was making Speke aware of the enemy when the time came. Somehow, if he could make enough noise and light, he could warn Speke. The only other place the Mexicans could be heading was Laredo – his own destination. Should he assume that, and race on ahead? His message was for the Governor. It must be important. The end of the day would tell.

In the Fortress, the Mexicans were being watched as well. Speke sat down with Liza and with Bill Cheto, who had run from his hotel in fear after it was burnt out by a bunch of bandits. He was worried sick about Emilio, and just as concerned about Bullhead, as he had not heard from him for too long.

'How many guns we got, Bill?' Speke asked as the three sat around the one table in the Speke home.

'Twenty men and three women . . . after that it's children. We have the sick ones . . . some could fire a gun, but not walk or run, that's for sure.' Liza explained.

'Look, Bernie, I've been runnin' ever since I can recall . . . I ran from Comanches and I ran from vigilantes once . . . now I'm running from a war but it seems like fate has me down to fight this time. I'm not runnin' any more.'

'Fine. Glad to hear that. But we need to think, and I only have one plan in my old head . . . seems to be that the Rangers will be headed this way soon. They will make for Laredo and Monterrey. Herrera has just one job . . . to clear out any nuisances before the Mexican army move north, this way . . . the Texans know that and they must be coming this way. We're on the track to Laredo, right?'

'Yes, Pa . . . it makes sense,' Liza said.

'Well, the best we can do is hold then, for as long as possible, and hope the Rangers arrive soon.' Speke wiped his brow. 'Give the women rifles, Liza . . . we have twenty-three fighters against . . . well, we don't rightly know how many!'

'There is one other possibility, Bernie . . . we run for Laredo now. We can cross the river . . . or we can get aboard the boats . . . it's getting dark.'

Speke thought this over. It could be done, that was for sure. But it was against the grain. Something inside him resisted the thought of running from a fight. 'The thing to remember, Bill, is that the longer we keep these roughnecks busy here, the less chance there is that they can fill up the ranks in the Mexican army.'

'You're right. I heard these Mexican troops . . . they line up in their thousands and they just run over you like an angry sea. Well, your pretty little fortress might just be a rock awkward enough to stall that tide a little, hey?' Bill Cheto said, with a touch of humour in his voice.

Less than a mile away, Herrera gathered his handful of leaders together – the men who led each band of fighters – and set out his thoughts. They sat around a fire and took some whiskey, passing it around as they listened.

'Now you see the situation. We are told that Speke has no more than maybe a dozen men fit to handle a weapon. We are a hundred and twenty. But they have a wall to hide behind. We can't do what our army does, and merely send in line after line of men, knowing that ten per cent will die . . . no, we thin them out first by rifle-fire, and then we charge, battering the gate. We send some men along the river bank, and others to attack the gate. We have one old wagon, and a log tied to that will hit the gate. It's only thin wood. No strength there. Now, drink, then sleep. Tomorrow we attack early, when they are wiping sleep from their eyes. The army are also close . . . we join them to go for Monterrey.'

Back in San Antonio, Pastor Jim had managed to talk Gillespie around to excusing Jack's failure to turn up for duty. The general opinion was that though he would miss the preparation, he would most likely learn by facing the guns and having to cope or go under.

The other recruits had a tough week ahead of them, learning to ride at speed and hang from their horses, Comanche-style, firing or throwing weapons while moving like the wind. Gillespie and Hays instilled in them the charge, not the fight from a dismount under cover, though that action would come. The Mexican cavalry would be fixed, predictable, open to be outmanoeuvred and outflanked. Mobility was the secret of success. Gillespie supervised every man's work, and Pastor Jim joined in, being no more than a raw recruit, just to learn what it was like. He claimed he might be there for the care of souls, but he had to be in the skin of those he rode with.

The pastor thought of Jack, and where he might be. The only reassurance was the thought that Gillespie's Rangers would be heading along the Rio Grande. The question was, would they find Jack Brady dead or alive, if they found him at all?

It was closing in on dusk when Emilio saw that the Mexicans were indeed joining someone else. He saw them set up camp not far from the river. He was a spy, he thought. It was time to do some real spying. His Spanish was his best asset now. Leaving his mare, but tucking the packet with the message into his belt, he walked closer to the encampment, lay down so he could see the remuda, and selected the man he would kill. He had his knife and revolver, and the knife was the only weapon possible. He slithered closer to the man on watch by the horses and moved behind him like a snake. In seconds, the man's throat was slit and the body pulled into cover. Then it was a change of clothes and Emilio Peters was a soldier of the Mexican army. Luck was on his side, he thought. Most of the soldiers were eating and drinking, and as he walked around, only one man greeted him and his Spanish was light and pleasant, fending off any further questions.

As night fell, Emilio found a spot where he could

listen to anything. He was just one of hundreds of men, all dragged into the army by conscription. They were peasants, food for the cannon, it was always said in Texas. He was not important enough to be noticed or to be questioned. He reasoned all this at least. But no sooner had he found out that the officer in command was talking to some other men outside a canvas cover spread on stakes, there was a shout and strong hands came around his throat. Then he was yanked roughly back with a cry of *tejano . . . tejano!*'

He was now held by several men and pushed towards the officer. The message was still in Emilio's belt. Everything he had been set to do would now be useless. The officer saw the packet and grabbed it. He ripped it open and read the message.

Emilio's heart sank. He had made every mistake in the book. He thought himself the worst messenger ever in the ranks of the Texan fighters. Now here was this jumped-up nobody acting like he was Napoleon. He sure loved his slice of power, even out in that backyard of his sad and lost country. There was nothing else to do but face it out. There would be no mercy.

'You have no chance of success . . . the Texans are on their way from San Antonio . . . one Ranger can whip ten of your excuses for fighting men!' Emilio always showed such spirit, and his reward was a slap across the face. 'Shut up, you dog!' the officer spat out.

'If I'm a dog, then I'm a cut above the rats who wear your uniform, mister!'

'Ah, a dog with some life in it! Amusing. . . .'

'A man, mister, a man.'

'Then you can prove that by dying like a man!'

'Sure can, Mexie!'

'Ah, so . . . you know, *señor*, spies are the worst, the lowest of one's enemies. I think that now we have this information, you are of no consequence. Unless, of course, you have more facts in your head and then naturally we would need those to be spilled out . . . may I persuade you to do that?' He was squat, heavy, moving slowly. He strode towards Emilio. 'You look like a *Mexicano* . . . yet you fight for Texas . . . for the United States. That makes you a traitor. Oh dear. Traitors are not long for this earth. But I'll speak to you in the morning. Tie him up and guard him!'

Emilio was dragged away, fastened to a stake and cracked unconscious by the slap of a rifle butt.

7

'Well that's it . . . no more hangin' around, Wate –
we get in there now.' Jack was watching the scene
where the bunch of Herrera's men were making
ready to move out. Wate was spitting out cold coffee.
'Just a minute, Brady. I never said I was signin' up for
no war. I mean, we stuck together after the bastards
jumped us . . . but now you're saying we need to ride
in there and join the Spekes?'

'Sure I'm saying that. Look, see the riverbank to
the north of the Fortress . . . we could ride in there
if we shift now, while the Mexies are preparing to
ride.' Jack pointed to the track by a rundown wharf
where Speke's boats were moored. 'That's a spot
where anyone could get in . . . the Mexies are too
dumb to see it. We have to act now.'

'But I have no fight with Mexico, Brady. Why
should I stand beside Speke and his little band of sui-
cidal Texans? If I have a home, it's back in Kansas,
but it's half a lifetime since I rode around anywhere

71

near there! Next thing I know, I'll be signed up for a soldier . . . anyway, how do you know we can ride in from the north, by the river? You got some special powers? Herrera's lot will have seen that as a weak spot in the defence, surely?'

'If they had, then men would be posted some-where near . . . and we would see them, right?'

Wate looked doubtful. He was thinking what a long ride it would be if he turned tail and went all the way back home.

Jack saddled up, packed everything into the pack, and then sprang up ready to ride. 'Evan Wate . . . here's me thinking we were partners! Look, what you win by fighting down there is something more than dollars. There's something at stake that can't be bought . . . freedom! I'm riding down there now, with or without you!' He dug his spurs into the belly of his Appaloosa and turned her around. He was soon riding away.

Wate made a quick decision, without thinking. He threw on his saddle and slid his rifle into place, and in a minute he followed, not thinking about any-thing – just doing what seemed right.

When Bernie Speke saw them riding along the bank, he shouted for a man to check their approach, and he stood in the way with his rifle pointed at Jack's head as he drew near enough to speak. Wate came close behind. Jack gave his name.

When Speke heard the name, he clambered down and walked quickly to meet the arrivals. There was a warm welcome.

'My God . . . the fighters from the Palace. I thought you was sworn enemies? Well, no matter . . . we need every gun we can get. You come to help I hope? We don't want no men just passin' through, you hear.'

Speke had the mounts taken care of and he led Jack and Wate to the barn, which was part eating room and part hospital. 'It's a sickroom in fact . . . but Liza says it's a hospital . . .' Speke said, as Liza heard her name and walked out to meet them.

It took no more than a few seconds for Jack Brady to sense the same feelings he had in the Palace to run across him. His look met Liza's eyes, and he was sure that she felt something for him. To Jack it was all new. Never before had he met a woman who knocked him out of his safe ways of thinking and into something that made his heart thump so that he felt it in his throat. They shook hands, and the touch of her palm sent Jack's body into an excited state that made him slur some words. Wate shook her hand too, and apologized for the scene in the hotel.

They ate some broth and bread, and had coffee that actually tasted like coffee. Liza was cook as well as nurse. 'My Liza, she does a wonderful job here, my friends . . . don't you, dear? I'm lost without you,' Bernie Speke said.

Jack, always with an interest in medicine, given to him by his father, asked to look at the sickroom. Liza was glad to have someone offer some help. She walked through to what was formerly a barn or store-room where provisions and equipment were kept for the boats, in the days some decades back when it looked like boats on the Rio Grande had a future.

'Mary there . . . she came in almost starved to death,' Liza said, pointing to a woman who was sleeping, curled into a ball like a baby; then there were two children, sitting together and sipping water. They were only half-dressed and stared with a vacant, lost expression, with no smiles on their thin faces. 'Jack, the other patient is a man with a fever, and there's little I can do. I've tried the patent med-icines that Pa bought back in Callego . . . seems like it is useless.'

'Liza, you're doing wonderful work here . . . I con-gratulate you.' Jack looked at her and wanted to say so much, but it was not the right time. The moment of relative quiet was broken by one of the children starting to cough, and Liza ran to him, picking him up and wiping his face clear of sweat.

Suddenly, there was a cry from the parapet. 'Now, see . . . we got company,' said Jack. 'I have to go. . . .'

'Take care!' Liza said, looking at him.

'I always do, Miss Speke.' He lifted his hat.

The parapet had filled up with armed men, some of them limping and one with his bandages flapping loose, hobbling on a walking stick. Bill Cheto was there, and he was as surprised as the others to see Jack and Wate together. Speke was snapping out orders. 'They're gonna run at the gate . . . see that wagon, and the log? They're all on horseback . . . I want three more men down at the gate. Roll a cart behind . . . strengthen it . . . move, move!' Some men ran down to follow orders.

'Now, every man left up here . . . let 'em get close . . . pick your man . . . I'll tell you when to fire. Right? Mister Wate, bein' long and thin is more risk . . . keep down, way down, out of sight . . . archin' low ain't easy but it's better than bein' a corpse!'

Herrera's band were in a line across the horizon, and they started to walk forward. They all carried rifles and pistols, and some of the Indians had lances and thick hide shields. It was a band of mixed colours across the east, with the sun now above them. The defenders were dazzled and had to shade their brows when they stared out at what was approaching. Then a voice from the southern end of the parapet screamed, 'Mister Speke . . . look, there's more!'

Heads turned to look. Sure enough, there was a solid rank of cavalry, and their raised sabres glinted in the sunlight. The defenders could just make out the blue jackets, the dark hats with the yellow band, and white cross-straps. They were closing in, and joining Herrera's men.

'Hell, there's hundreds of 'em!' Bill Cheto shouted.

'Well there's twenty-three of us, and we don't have to scale a wall,' Speke laughed back.

'They appear to have no artillery,' Jack said to Speke.

'Yeah, but look behind . . . see any infantry?'

The answer was no. It was all going to depend on a charge.

'I want anybody available down at that gate!' yelled Bernie Speke, and his daughter heard the appeal. She ran out and looked around. In the sick-room there were three men who, though fevered, could hold a revolver or a knife. Along the river there were some boatmen who had been detailed to watch the north. It was a risk, but they were told the situation and they ran to the parapet.

The Mexican commander, Captain Silveras, had joined Herrera and taken command. He was a thin, unpleasant man in his fifties, with no humour and a sulky, morose disposition. His face and appearance had all the hallmarks of the dandy. He took a long time to prepare his beard, hair and moustache for the day and acted as if he was capable of comparison with the great military leaders in history. He quoted them at times and took volumes of military history on campaign, carried by skivvies, of course.

That morning, before gathering the men for the planned assault on the Fortress, he had left Emilio in the care of two guards, aiming to take his prisoner to Monterrey where no doubt, as a spy, the man would be a valuable subject for a more than energetic interrogation.

'Left to my own actions,' he told his aide de camp, 'I would have the man shot immediately. But no doubt he knows a lot about the enemy's intentions.'

By nine, after a substantial breakfast, he was leading the battalion out towards the river. When he saw the state of the Fortress, he laughed, and when he met with Herrera to discuss the attack, he was dismissive of any serious argument about the enemy. They were to be brushed aside in one swoop.

He was beside Herrera, staring at the adobe walls and the wooden gate. 'Oh dear me, Koni, have we ever had a simpler task? How many guns?'

'We think twenty. There are women and children in there, too.'

'Well, they may be left alone, of course. They will follow us to Laredo . . . cooks and nurses!'

After another half an hour of checking weapons and horses, the line was ready for the charge. Silveras sent his men forward, sabres raised, at first walking. From the parapet, Speke's company of assorted civilians took their positions and were set to fire when ordered.

'Remember . . . when I give the order . . . till then, wait and wait!' Speke said.

The Mexicans' wagon, with a man at the reins and two horses pulling, made towards the gate. As they neared the hundred yard mark, covering fire came in a volley from a line of Herrera's men who had galloped behind and taken positions where they could see the gate. Bullets ripped into the wood. Behind the gate, half a dozen men and women stood by the wagon with pistols and knives ready. One had a

Mexican sword captured in the man's last confrontation with the marauders of the border.

The wagon closed on the gate, and the driver threw himself clear, rolling in the dust and staggering to his feet. Bill Speke took aim at him and put a slug in his head. The man folded like a jackknife and hit the earth.

The log shook the gate and splintered the wood but did not break it. Silveras let out a curse. But his line was now still firm and resolved to have an effect.

The line trotted now, a little faster. A voice shouted something that the defenders could not hear nor understand, and then, a few hundred yards out, the line quickened and sabres were jabbed forward. Some had rifles ready. Some had lances.

They kicked on, and shrieks of encouragement were given to the expectant air. Above them, Bernie Speke rapped out the word 'Fire!' The effect was deadly. A dozen riders fell back, rolling off their mounts with grunts and screams. Other men turned their horses to the side and rode along the parapet, firing upwards. Their bullets hit home and floored some of the defenders. Then the line of cavalry wheeled around and turned, riding back to come in a second time.

There were a few minutes now for Speke, Cheto and the rest to make ready for the next attack. Two men were dead on the wooden floorboards. A third was wounded in the arm, and Liza came up a ladder, crept along and led the man out to the safety of the barn behind, helped by Jack to take the man's weight as he staggered to his feet.

'Here they come again! Same as last time, men . . . fire when I say!' Bernie Speke cried out.

The line gathered again. Other teams of men, on foot, were roping the wagon and pulling it back from the gate. But the log was embedded in the wood. On came the line of blue and red. Silveras shouted out like a man possessed, and Herrera rode out to join his own men, who were working on the wagon.

The cavalry cantered again, and rifles were lifted. Sabres flashed and glinted. The pace quickened. Closer and closer they came. Jack, Wate, Cheto and Speke were men who knew guns and killing. The others were new to the art of death. Barrels fixed on their targets and again the cry of 'Fire!' snapped out from Speke's mouth above the noise of the charge.

Shots rang out. Jack used both his five-barrel Patersons now, as he was close enough to see the Mexicans well. He crawled along, taking shots from behind the wooden crates that had been piled on the parapet as turrets. Evan Wate, with only one hand able to shoot, was sitting lower, taking fewer but accurate shots, and doing some considerable damage to the Mexican line.

Bill Cheto was hit and fell back, dropping off the parapet like a stone, and two others were killed on the defence line.

Again the cavalry line wheeled away and

retreated. They galloped back towards their commander.

Jack ran down to look at Cheto, who was lying on the earth below, still as stone. Liza had got to him first, felt his pulse and then simply said: 'He's gone.' She covered the body with a coat. 'He'll never see his Emilio again . . . he shouldn't have come here . . . the fool!' Jack wanted to hold her, keep her safe and close. But he was wanted back above. 'Here they come again!' shouted Speke.

But when Jack reached the parapet he saw that this was not the case. The line of men stood and looked at each other, and then, as they saw the Mexicans move backwards, they raised their hats and cheered.

Their joy was foolish and risky. A shot rang out, and a bullet hit Bernie Speke at the shoulder. He put a hand to the wound and fell back, rocking against the adobe wall, before sliding down to the wooden board. He was still awake and coping with the pain when Jack went down to help, picking the man up and walking towards the sickroom. Bernie had one thing on his mind, and he said it to a man he was starting to trust, 'Brady . . . take care of my daughter. Her man will want to see her alive when he gets here. ... .'

'Her man?' Jack asked, feeling a shock run through his body.

'Sure . . . she's spoken for . . . officer in the Rangers, name of Emilio Peters. God knows where he is, but his thoughts will be with her right now. . . .'

Jack Brady had just started to allow some thoughts and feelings to reach up to the surface of his being, as if they had lain down in the murky darkness of somewhere he thought did not exist. Now there was only darkness again. But still he felt that he needed the man's daughter. He said nothing except, 'I'll look after her.'

8

Silveras decided to attack the Fortress again the next day. There were heavy losses in the first charges, and there were wounded men staggering back, away from the day's scene of carnage. Herreras and his men were left with the rest of Silveras's men while the captain rode back to find out more about Emilio. He knew that he had a valuable prisoner, a man who surely knew a great deal about the Rangers to the north. His superiors in Monterrey would be very pleased to learn about the manpower of the San Antonio Volunteers and the Rangers themselves.

When he reached his camp, Emilio was eating and sitting up, though still fastened to the stake. His guards were laughing and joking with him. 'This man . . . he speaks Spanish . . . he even tells stories in Spanish, Captain,' said the guard in charge, who stood and saluted Silveras, as did the other two guards behind.

'Very interesting, I'm sure, but he will have no

more food until I give the order!' Silveras kicked the plate of food away, out of Emilio's hands.

'Bring him into the sun ... tie him over there, where he will burn. I'm resting for a while. When I come back, he will answer questions or be left to bake while we move on!'

Emilio was taken from shade into the scorching sun and tied hands and feet. Then he was left to wriggle where he could, but he could not stand. He felt more like a snake than a man. But he managed to find a spot with some cover, and the guards, kindly towards him now, let him stay there. One brought him water, tipping the canteen into the prisoner's parched mouth.

There was only one thing on Emilio's mind now: to get out of there, and fast.

'Our only hope is your boat, Bernie!' Jack Brady told the wounded man lying back on the makeshift straw bed. Liza was cleaning the wound on the shoulder. 'Bernie ... you have that row-boat, with the little cabin. All the people left could get aboard now, and I'll get her down to Laredo. Come on!'

'Maybe ... but get this damned bullet out first ... now!' Bernie said, taking the whiskey being offered by his daughter. 'How many men left ... fighting men?'

'Nine men armed. We lost one by the gate. Three women also armed. Five children here with the wounded. Five wounded including you,' Jack said, looking around. 'They won't come again until tomorrow, Bernie. We have time.'

Wate, standing close by, didn't like it. 'If we get on that heap of old wood, the Mexies will see us from the bank, pick us off. It's just a row-boat, Brady. How many men need to row it?'

'Six men could do it.' Bernie said. 'Get the slug out, for Christ's sake . . . and yes, let's use the boat. You put the plan into action, tall man!'

'I think it's foolishness, but what the hell, I'm here, somehow stuck in somebody else's fight, and I can't just ride home. Might as well play the brainless soldier!' He set about gathering everybody to explain the plan of escape.

Jack had seen bullets extracted on more than one occasion, and Liza had a few medical tools. She washed the pliers as best she could, while Jack gave Bernie more whiskey. 'I think it's in deep, Bernie.' Jack said, 'But I'll be as quick as I can.'

As the sick behind were helped to gather their belongings and be guided out into the yard, Jack set to work, with Liza standing by him. She whispered, 'Brady . . . save him please! He's my Pa and I love him. We been through so much. . . .'

Jack held the mouth of the wound back to allow room for the pliers. Bernie winced and bit on the old hammer-handle he had between his teeth. There was thick muscle to work through and Bernie was almost wretching and squealing with pain as the teeth of the pliers went deeper. Then Jack said, 'I

can feel the edge of the slug . . . just a little more . . .
hold on, there Bernie.' There was a lurch of the
patient's body and his head rocked back and forth,
before he lost consciousness.

Jack had hold of the bullet and pulled hard now,
knowing that the pain could not be felt. In another
few seconds, the bullet was out and tossed onto a tin
plate. He was sweating with the fear of possibly
killing the old man. He knew that every kind of work
like this could rupture an artery. Pa had told him
some useful things when the two of them had gone
out on calls in the buggy, back when things were
good for the Brady family.

Liza put her arms around Jack and squeezed him,
thanking him again and again. When she let him go
and stood away again, he felt a warm sensation go
through him. Her closeness reminded him of how
much he wanted her. But there was no time to waste.
A wound like that was still a dangerous thing.
Whiskey was poured on it. The bustle of packing up
and walking out the back towards the boat went on,
as dusk approached.

Bernie slept a while, mercifully, and after several
hours of carrying the wounded aboard, and then
essential provisions, there were just Jack and Evan
Wate on the parapet. Looking out at the lights from
the Mexican fires. Wate asked: 'Do you think they
saw us . . . heard us, Brady?'

'I pray not. Around twenty folk on a row-boat,
dragging every scrap of food and clothing they have,

well that makes some noise. But you did a good job, Sergeant Wate!' Jack enjoyed the joke. Wate did a mock salute.

'I'm officially a signed-up Volunteer, with Hays himself in command. Problem is, I strayed from my platoon, or whatever we are!'

'Well now, you're all makin' me feel like a Texan!' Wate said. 'Now, look out there . . . they're watchin' us right now.'

'Sure they are. Now, in maybe another hour, we get the boat out on the river, ever so steady . . . we got thirty foot of old wood and it might make some noise in the night as we swish along. What do you reckon?'

'Brady, one thing I never was . . . a sea-faring man, nor even a river-farin' man. If there's a God up there, like my pa always told me, we better do some special prayin' to the man!'

Jack gave a wry smile.

Silveras was up and about his business again, but he had left the fighting men in his charge out in the position overlooking the Fortress. He was concentrating on his prisoner. What he didn't know was that Emilio had worked and worked at the ropes holding him, so that his hands were nearly free. But for the time being, with Silveras standing over him, Emilio fixed his mind on looking helpless as a new-born foal.

'Now, *tejano* spy, I am to assume that you wish to

preserve your rag-tag little life? Of course, of course
... well, if that is so, you must first tell me how
many Texans are massing at San Antonio? I know
they will be coming south towards Monterrey, and
to Laredo ... my own army awaits them, and we
outnumber them by around eight to one, I would
say. If you bear all this in mind, you will see that the
situation is hopeless. The States have their dragoons, I know. They are all preening themselves
after Palo Alto ... but our ranks grow more very
day ... we have enough men to block out the
horizon when a battle is coming ... you understand? So your Volunteers are adding to the enemy
and we wish to keep our superiority. I need
numbers!'

The guards sat their prisoner upright, and he
spoke, in spite of the fatigue creeping into him.
'Listen, Captain ... I am also an officer. I'm not just
a drifter joined up to make a few new amigos. Oh
no, I've studied the wars of the past ... as I know
you have. I know that numbers are not everything.
See this grey coat ... and these chaps ... the stripes
on the breeches? This is a uniform ... of sorts. It
means we have a force of fighting men ... we are
not roughnecks out to cut up the peace in the
streets.'

'All very fine. But I still want numbers.'

'Let's say eighty. That's as good a lie as any.'

'Oh *madre mio*, you try to be hard!' He took his
pistol and swung the butt at the back of Emilio's

head. He yelled and fell to the dust again.

'We'll talk again later.' Silveras walked away, to swallow some wine and decide what to do next.

The boat was ready now. Rifles had been propped on the walls, so that the attackers would think there were still defenders inside. The sick were placed in the one wooden hut in the centre of the row-boat, which made do for a cabin of sorts. The rest of the craft was open to the elements, and the six oarsmen were at their positions. They had no weapons but rifles and revolvers. Jack took the prow and Wate the stern. One man and three women held rifles and spread along the sides.

'We're hardly a battleship, but we're heading for Laredo and that ain't too far,' Jack said to Bernie, who had now come round again and was sitting up in the corner of the hut, full of pain but glad to be alive and well enough to talk tactics to his new friend. 'Look, Jack, we got about thirty miles to go I guess. When will they see that we've gone?'

'About early dawn. They'll have crawlers, listeners, slithering up close to listen. Then there are their glasses . . . they'll see empty spaces . . . too many.'

Wate sighed. 'My God! They'll soon be on our backside, Brady. We can't pick up any speed. We have to rely on six men pulling a thirty-foot craft. They could take us in a few minutes . . . just blast us with firepower!'

'Yeah . . . which is why we need a good start . . . get

maybe two or three miles out before dawn.'

They moved out in the moonlight, rowing with an action slow as mule with a stack of hay on his back.

9

Gillespie and the Volunteers were finally making ready to pull out of San Antonio. Eighty men had learned how to ride at speed and shoot, duck to swing a sabre blade, fire a rifle from the shoulder. They had been starved, shouted and enslaved into fighters, the reasoning from John Hays at the top being that a real fighter goes hell for leather, instils fear, and then, between fights, stays away from being vulnerable. There was a bunch of men lined up in the morning sun when Gillespie rode along them and made everything clear.

'Now listen, you men. You came to fight for Texas . . . you are now fighting for the United States as well. We will be meeting up with the dragoons somewhere close to Laredo, but our main orders are to reach and take control of Laredo until the States army gathers and moves on south. What we are to do is hit hard on the roving scouts and marauders of the Mexies between here and the Rio Grande. The more we give them trouble, the less they will complement the Mexican army . . . and they're not short of men as it is. Now, we move fast and we hit hard . . . even the pastor here is riding with us. With the Almighty on our side, how can we fail?'

Pastor Jim showed his amusement and there was laughter along the line. They had grown to like the pastor's company. A young padre was not what they expected. In their minds, they had seen an old-timer who would throw sermons and sober advice at them all day. What they got with Pastor Jim was a friend who spoke straight and honest. He was going to fight alongside them too, in a war he saw as a just cause, for the right.

'Now men . . . Texans and friends of Texas . . . We could meet Comanches, *comancheros* or Mexies . . . it don't matter. Whatever they are, we go at 'em and hit 'em hard as a bison crackin' at a gate!' Gillespie dismissed them, to make their final preparations.

Emilio was now sure that one more pull at the rope behind him that held his wrists together would set him free. It was dark enough to dart out into the night and put some distance between the soldiers and himself. The one problem was the guard who had been assigned to sit with him. He was awake, and drinking some wine. Emilio dragged his feet along a line of dust and stirred up a little cloud. The sentry saw it and turned to him. Emilio licked his lips with his tongue and smiled.

'*Muy buen, señor* . . . a little only. Here. . . .' The soldier knelt to give him the drink and, with one last yank of his hands, Emilio was free to swing a punch. It had to be accurate, and it had to be quick as a rattler's stab. His fist cracked the man on his temple, and as he lurched back, another punch knocked him flat out and unconscious.

'My apologies . . . you are a good man,' Emilio whispered, as he went to work untying the ropes at his feet. Then he took the man's bayonet. He looked around like a hunted animal in the dark. All was silent. He moved slow as a lizard in the sun, then found a shadow and cowered down for a second to look around again before walking, still bent forward, out into the cooling night.

He ached; he felt the pain of the assaults on his now exhausted body, but he had no option but to get out into the dark where he would be safe. His mind thought how close he must be to Liza. Inside him, a voice urged him to go to her, to run to the river and shout for her at the Fortress. Please God, he thought, let her be safe. He had not been with her for two months, such had been the revolution in life that war brings. *Let her be safe . . . I beg of you Lord . . . She is gentle and good . . . she is to be my wife . . . protect her . . . send her a guardian to watch over her . . . hear my prayer. . . .*

He pushed himself on, into the night, with the sounds of the creatures who relished the darkness heard all around him. When the tiredness seemed to take him like some giant grip of a hunter, he sat still and silent in a shadowy hole. If they followed him, he would need the guile of a hunted fox. He felt his legs growing so weak that they were soft as pudding. There was no food in him. His belly spasmed with hunger. He felt that it was inevitable he should fall and give in, fold up like a beaten nag. But somehow the strength came and came again, as he pushed on, sensing the way to the river.

If he could just make it to the river, he had a chance. Along the river, he could get to where Liza was. That thought held him together and he found the strength to keep on walking.

On the row-boat the light was slowly streaking across the horizon. The rowers had taken short rest periods, and Jack and Wate had stepped in for a while as they ate and moved their stiff muscles. In the cabin the sick had managed to sleep, albeit fitfully. Liza had been able to sleep on and off through the night, always on the edge of awareness, in case a voice cried out for help.

Her father, with his wound bound and the shoulder strapped so it was hard to move it, could now sit and do what he liked to do – give orders. He was now out of the cabin and sat on a spar in the centre of the boat, looking hard at the riverbank. Jack came to sit with him as the boat glided stealthily eastwards towards Laredo.

'Son, we get there, then it's all well. You hear? I

know the town. The Texans will have it . . . your man Gillespie, and Ben McCulloch . . . if they got it, they'll fight like rabid dogs to keep it. I believe we won them some time . . . then there's the States men, the dragoons and rifles – they have to be coming south by now surely. Last I heard, they were fifty miles above San Antonio.'

'Don't fret Mr Speke . . . rest up. You got a bad wound there,' Jack said, looking at the dried blood on the bandage. 'Best you do nothing strenuous. I'm praying that the whiskey will do the job . . . keep it clean.'

'You a medical man, son?'

'Son of a doctor . . . I watched him a lot.'

'You got a sweetheart back home, Brady?'

It was a question that hit Jack like an axe. He felt himself shudder and then feel a kind of emptiness overpower him. 'Well, Mister Speke . . . interesting that you should ask, because recently I been feeling something real deep for a woman . . . but it is not to be. I guess fate has meant me to ride alone . . . I done that for fifteen years since I left home.' He was seeing Liza's face as he spoke.

Speke knew nothing of what Jack really meant.

'Well Brady, my friend, the question is, how long before some Mexie cavalry come stormin' along that river bank and start shootin' at us? An hour? Two?'

'We can guess all day. Best thing, as we know it's to be the north bank, let me and Wate, with the two women shooters you got, settle into the port side and wait for trouble.'

'Fine . . . me as well, son. I can sit and pull a trigger.'

'I don't think so, Mister Speke. I think you need to lie low . . . eat what you can . . . get strong.'

'That's the biggest load of hoss droppings I ever heard! I'm fit to fire a rifle, and I got one right here. Help me get over to that spot on the stern. . . .'

There was no use arguing with Bernie Speke. He was made of something hard as teak and impossible to talk down once his mind was set.

Meanwhile, as the shooters settled into position, taking the coffee Liza brought out to them, and the rowers now pushed themselves in spite of their increasing exhaustion, the day grew hotter and the light dazzled everyone. By midday, Speke could see that they would have to rest, or some would die of the heat and the exertion. He shouted for Jack to drop the anchor – a home-made affair as heavy as a work-horse, and the rowers gratefully stopped arching their aching bodies and sat back, fighting for normal breathing. The punishing sun showed no mercy.

'We stop here for a while,' Speke said. 'We take some food and water . . . then I reckon we can do another five miles . . . we done five through the night. But we have to rest regular . . . see? Six men workin' like this – well, it's asking for a slow and nasty death. You'll dry up like sagebrush and be cut just as loose from life. Now drink . . . and keep the hats on your heads!'

As they started to take water in mugs from Liza, Evan Wate pointed back along the bank and shouted, 'Dust . . . I see dust! Back there . . . behind us.'

10

A strong hand grasped his collar and he was too weak to turn and speak. It was a tanned, gnarled hand – the hand of a farmer or a fighter. He was almost too exhausted to speak, and he fought for each word he managed to utter. 'I am Emilio Peters, Texas Rangers . . . who are you?'

He was looking up at a weathered, tanned face with a straw hat above it, and as his eyes gradually focused, he saw a blue and white bandana and a patterned shirt, with a flapping breastplate of bone. 'Call me Tammy. Toma Lori is my real name, but the troopers make their own words, an old army thing. I work as scout for the United States Army . . . I found you just in time, brother.' The man called out and soon another man joined them, and Emilio was lifted onto their pack horse.

'This is John Four Tongues. We're Tonkawa. That's in the blood,' Tammy said, 'But today, and with this trouble shaking the land, we're United

States soldiers. You need help.'

They tried to move out, with Emilio nodding forward on the pack horse, just coping with the reins. He felt so weak that he feared he would not stay in the saddle. But the Tonkawas could see this, and the plan was abandoned. They sat Emilio down in some shade. 'I will go to the captain and tell him . . . you stay with our friend, John.' Tammy said.

'I was taking a message to Laredo . . .' Emilio said. 'Tell your captain. It was about Mexicans moving south from the Pecos . . . in force.'

'We have seen them, worry not, Emilio. Try to rest. John will sit with you.'

Tammy rode off. John, who was short and light, had a check smock over his breeches, and long hair. His face was pock-marked with what looked like wounds, and he saw Emilio staring. 'Comanches . . . they did this. The Tonkawa are not too happy when they meet Comanches . . . time has made us friends and enemies. They like torture. I was lucky to live.'

'Well we both have the same enemies now . . . the Mexicans have many men,' Emilio said.

'Yes, but you are not to fret about that. You need food. Here.' John held out some hardtack. 'Eat . . . and sip water from this canteen. Keep sipping.'

'Where have you been doing your scouting, my friend?'

'We have ridden many miles . . . the regiment is a few miles north – The Regiment of Mounted Rifles – good men, all blooded fighters. We're joining others to defend Laredo. There's a big fight coming.'

When Tammy rode back, they could see from his face that there was trouble. He dismounted, ran to them, and said, 'Follow me . . . up this slope. . . .' They helped Emilio up, and when they were high enough to see across the next valley, Tammy pointed. 'Look . . . *comancheros*. Maybe three hundred I would say.'

'Heading south east . . . Laredo again. They are all going to Laredo,' John said.

They sat down. Tammy wiped the sweat from his brow. 'See, our regiment must be only a mile behind. The Mexicans are gathering all their allies. A big fight is coming.'

Emilio thought about his message, and wondered how important it was that it was now in the hands of Silveras. But after all, it concerned the Rangers and the Volunteers, and they would be not too far north by now, he thought.

John took out some field glasses and watched the comancheros. 'Hey . . . some riders have come to meet them. Wait . . . what are they doing? Oh, one is pointing to the river. What lies to the west . . . on the river?'

Emilio knew the answer to that question only too well. It was the Fortress and his Liza. 'I know exactly what is there, John. They need our help, and right now! Can you have your regiment turn to follow these men we are watching?

'If you can do that, you could save many lives.'

'Tammy . . . ride hard to the regiment. Tell them to head for the river. We will go ahead now.'

Tammy went off at speed, knowing he had only a short distance to go, so that if his stirring the dirt caught the eye of the *comancheros*, he would be with the soldiers long before they caught up with him.

As for Emilio, he started to pray as he and John Four Tongues set out for the river.

On the row-boat, the sun was now up and all heads turned to look north, to see who the riders were who came towards their stern. Bernie Speke was sleeping, after being given a draught to knock him out. The pain in his wound was too much to tolerate. Jack was with Liza at the port side, squatting by the other armed men. He was close to her, and felt the need to take care of her. There was danger coming near, and there she was, so young, and she could not be his. 'You look at me as if you're doing an inspection!' she laughed.

'Maybe I am . . . but I know you're spoken for, Liza. I know about your man, in the Rangers.'

A look of fear crossed her face like a shadow on a warm day. 'Yes, my Emilio is with the Rangers, but they are outnumbered, I know. I'm praying for him to be safe. But you . . . look at you. Surely another calling is for you . . . something more than a gunman.'

'What do you mean?'

'A man of medicine, you fool . . . you have a

special ability . . . a golden touch with those hands. Haven't you seen how skilled you are at saving life? Yet they all speak of you as a killer.'

He was shocked. His mind roved through his memory, and he saw his father's face. Then thought of the day that he had watched his pa save a man's life. He had fallen in the street and was clutching his chest. His father had worked on him and snatched the man from death.

'You have surely saved my father's life. I am eternally grateful, Jack Brady!' Her smile melted something in him, some deep resistance in him that had pushed away any expression of true feelings. Emotion, he had come to learn, increases the chances of defeat.

Someone called out, 'Heads down . . . they're shooting!' A bullet cracked into the cabin behind Jack and Liza, and they went lower down, ducking behind the boxes and planks they had loaded for cover before setting out. Jack knew the riders would move much quicker than the boat, and sure enough, the defenders started shouting out warnings as everyone on board scurried across to the port side. There, they saw around a dozen riders, going along the bank, pausing to shoot after moving slightly ahead of the craft.

'We'll have to stop!' Wate shouted. 'We need every gun we got!'

Jack Brady took charge, risking the dangers of the situation by running around, giving orders. He could see that the best move was to make for a bend up ahead where there was a high ridge.

'No, I want everyone over to the starboard . . . around three hundred yards and we got a bend, and a low bank we can run on . . . we got no chance on the boat!'

The men rowing turned to the right, and the distance from the attackers steadily increased. Everyone stood by to jump off when they crossed to the shallow water before the bend.

'We make for the higher ground. Liza and Wate . . . carry Bernie . . . I'll cover your backs.'

The boat was further and further from the shooters across the river, and they were now frustrated. More of their force began to arrive and gather, waiting for orders. When the boat landed, hitting the sand and stones, Jack had everyone on shore and walking upwards towards the bluff. If they could make it up there, they could withstand attack. The only problem would be food and water. Under the shadow of the higher ground, Jack had everyone stop and sit under cover.

'Right everyone . . . fact is, they have to cross to come at us. We have the advantage. We have some time, as they're waiting for their full body of men and the commander to join them, right? I say we make some defences. We crowd into that space, where we have rocks in front, and the ridge behind.'

He was right. It took a few hours for first Herrera and then Silveras, to arrive. Nobody could give any orders until Silveras was with them. Herrera knew the land well. He saw the long stretch ahead, and he knew that Laredo was only an hour's ride from the bend. He stamped the ground with frustration. They had to act now, because he thought the Speke party might make for Laredo on land if they had a head start. He took out his frustration on the men, rapping out trivial and unnecessary orders. All eyes from the Mexican force gathered there were on the left bank, glaring across at the little group who were surely cornered and terrified. But they had to wait.

Herrera counted the minutes, stamped around, walking back and forth like a caged cat; the prey were in sight. They were almost helpless. Now precious time was passing, uselessly. It was always the same with the Mexican army, he thought: everything had to be done according to rules and regulations, and everything meticulously checked, ranks observed, orders cautiously conceived. No way to fight a war, he thought. Then he heard the riders. Finally, there was Silveras, leading the rest of the battalion. He snapped out orders, then asked for a report on the situation. He then did what a leader should always do – gave orders to Herrera and to his officers, who sat around as the light of the afternoon began to fade. He could see Herrera's face and he knew the brooding discontent it showed.

'Now, the information I have is that there is to be

an assault on Laredo. We have orders to regain the place. It was taken by the States and Texans, and they have no idea what strength we have . . . allies are heading to Laredo as I speak to you now. We are to join them immediately. It seems that the States forces are still moving south, recruited from a long, long way north . . . I've heard of Indiana men and Illinois . . . it is imperative that we strike now before they are stronger. General Arista, shamed at Palo Alto, looks to regain his reputation. Now, what do we find at this important point in the campaign? Stand around and talk more tactics? Well no more. Soon it will be dark. We cross the river tomorrow, and we sweep them away. I want everyone killed . . . women as well as men, understand? But first, we need boats, and there are some down the river at the maniac Speke's place. The horses can't get over there, and we can't swim over . . . so we need to move quickly. I want the best twenty men for rowing the boats down to the maniac's place now. . . .'

The soldiers looked at their friends' faces, expressing doubt, but orders were orders. One officer detailed the men to ride down the riverbank and bring the boats.

'Now, do we know who is over there in that sandy little creek?' Silveras asked the officers. One man said, 'Sir, there is a very tall man . . . good shot . . . and another sharp gunman. They have done some slaughter of our men. Also maybe three or four women . . . some sick, too. They carry some . . . obviously sick and wounded.'

'That is not important! We attack as soon as the boats arrive. Now I want a close observation of them . . . all night. I want three men over there, posted for constant watch, clear?' It was, and the men moved off to their places or to rest.

As this conference was in progress, two riders arrived at the Fortress. They saw that it was deserted, and thought the worst. They were John and Emilio, and as they saw the abandoned fort and sensed the uneasy silence, they walked their mounts inside, expecting not only to see corpses, but to expect trouble. Their eyes searched every window and doorway, every wall and gate. But there was nothing and nobody.

'If these people were killed . . . they are in the river, Mr Emilio,' John Four Tongues said. 'Were they known to you . . . *amigos?*'

Emilio struggled to find words, but finally he said, 'One was my future wife.'

They walked everywhere. As there were no signs of ruin and destruction, it took some figuring to imagine what had happened. But John spoke, as they stood on the shore of the Rio Grande, saying softly, 'My friend, I think they sailed away . . . downstream. God help them!'

'You could be right, John. There is hope for Liza . . . there is! Come on . . . we're needed!' They knew

105

they had to ride, even as darkness fell; for Emilio
Peters, he had to believe that the first light would be
one of hope.

11

That night, it was clear to Bernie Speke, now feeling much better and able to advise on what to do in the position his group were in, that the Mexicans were going to cross the river and come at them. It was a question of when. Bernie and Liza sat with Jack and Wate, but they had not made a fire. Luck was with them, as it was a dark night, but not too cool. Their only food was hardtack and some bread that had been thrown into a bag in their escape.

'We could run to Laredo now ... go into the night, follow the river on this bank ...' Bernie said, but he was cut off by Evan Wate. 'Sir, I have to say that in my experience, it's best to stay and fight in a case like this. We have backs to the wall, sure ... but we have plenty of men and women with guns, and we have a stock of cartridges ... best of all we have a defensive position. Point is, this is not even my fight. I don't belong here. But you're in a tight spot, and I never ran from a fight, yet.'

Jack Brady was listening and thinking, chewing over the situation. 'Now listen . . . we don't wait . . . we get to Laredo now! If we don't, then we'll be attacked by so many Mexies we'll be like a sugar pudding with a swarm of bees on us. They have to have transport, right? That's why they can't come now. They're watching us, sure, through the glasses, but that's in the dark. I say we move out now. Even a steady walk will take us to Laredo by dawn. We got two folks who can't walk . . . so we make stretchers and carry them. We agreed?'

It needed Bernie Speke's nod, and he got it. In no time, they were all busy. The stretchers were made with cut boughs from the string of old and half-dead cottonwoods, with some of Liza's bandages used for the ties. Bernie could walk, though slowly. Two men carried the sacks of food that Liza had brought. Now, in the thick of the night, it was time to move out. Jack and Wate walked at the back, their eyes scanning the darkness, looking for movement.

Jack knew that they would have to skirt some ridges. The river was far from straight, and at Dos Piedras, that he had seen a way ahead earlier that day, if they really had to stop, there was a defensible headland. Progress was achingly slow; though mostly flat, the earth was soft and walking in sandy soil was a strain on the legs. But Jack hung on to the fact that there was no way that the Mexicans could cross the Rio Grande on that stretch with horses.

'What happens if you're wrong, Brady?' Evan Wate asked.

'We blast them . . . go down fighting like I always knew I would!'

Out on the plain, the Rangers with the Volunteers had ridden out of San Antonio and the scouts from the States regiment had found them. Pastor Jim, riding with Gillespie, had been desperate for news of Jack, and also of Liza, thinking of his promise to Bullneck. Days had seemed like weeks as he had waited for the Gillespie outfit to hit the track. Out on the open range, the Volunteers had tasted their first experience of riding together, as a unit. Gillespie had a bunch of veteran Texans with him up front, and they were the first to see the States scouts riding up to them, led by Tammy.

Soon the story was told. Pastor Jim felt the burden of worry fall from him when Tammy related the encounter with Emilio. But this was followed by more concern when he learned that the kid had ridden out again. But nothing was to be done. Gillespie and the States Rifles had to make straight for Laredo, which was to be held, as a base for future plans to take Monterrey.

'Sorry, Jim, but we can't afford to go chasin' after the boy. Orders are orders, and it's Laredo . . . the Mexicans are gatherin' there for a siege.'

It was all in the hands of God, Jim thought. As for Liza, the boy's future wife, well she was in the

Almighty's care, too. He had never felt so helpless. The one consolation in his mind was that he knew Jack Brady was there someplace, and he would do everything a man could do to keep folk safe.

Around thirty miles from Laredo, the Rifles and the Volunteers joined up. Gillespie shook hands with Colonel Calhoun of the Rifles. The entire force moved to Laredo, and everyone along the river was left to do the best they could.

Emilio was riding with one of the best scouts that the States had. John Four Tongues was well aware that the Mexicans were on the river, and they would be close. In that same dark, all-enveloping darkness, he and Emilio went south, expecting to see the rowboat soon. But John could hear things that were beyond Emilio's senses. He motioned for them to duck off the river track and get cover. They had been behind rocks only a few minutes when the riders from Silveras' Mexicans rode past.

'They go to the Fortress, Emilio. Only one reason for that . . . boats.' John said. 'There's nothing else there that they could want.' They soon worked out that Silveras was a short way down river. Emilio was thinking the worst. 'So, we found nobody at the Speke place . . . they took a boat. Now, I figure they ran into Silveras. My poor Liza is there, John, she's there, with the animal Silveras most likely shutting her up a prisoner . . . or worse!'

'That is bad thinking, my friend. A man looks to

the sun even in a storm.'

'John, I hope and pray that you're right. You Tonkawas know a thing or two then?'

'We know when the mind itself can be its strongest enemy.'

Still keeping the horses still, and in cover, they remained there for a while, to think through the situation. It was clear that Speke and Liza were downriver; there was only one plan – to track along the bank, at a short distance, and let John do what he did best, by riding around and seeing what was happening.

It didn't take long for them to size up the situation. They had covered a mile or so, when they caught sight of two boats coming down river. They could plainly see that the Mexicans were on board, and the craft were shifting at considerable speed.

'Laredo again, John. Everybody is moving down to Laredo,' Emilio said.

'Yes my friend. I know this river, and if your friends are down there, then they will very soon find these boats at their backs. But what can two men do? We are helpless.'

There were around twenty men on each boat. Most were rowing, and others stood with rifles ready. Emilio racked his brain to try to think of what could stop them. Everything was building up, signifying big trouble for Liza and Speke somewhere down from where he stood, feeling helpless. The boats passed, and Emilio and John jogged along behind, keeping out of sight. The long night went on, and only when there were signs of the first light of dawn did the boats come alongside Silveras and Herrera, with their men.

Emilio and John saw then what was happening. The soldiers clambered aboard, so that both craft were packed with fighting men. But one of Silveras' scouts ran down the slope of the bank, shouting, 'They've gone! Speke has gone. . . .'

Suddenly it was all clear. The chase was on for Speke and the remnants of his Fortress, and Liza would be among them. John looked at Emilio and both thought the same thing. Emilio put it simply, 'They're on foot . . . over there!'

The next hour looked like being the final one on earth for the hunted over the Rio Grande. It was no use praying for the States army or the Texans to come. John knew that they would be in Laredo by now.

'All we can do is follow on, and then pick a few off,' Emilio said.

'Not quite . . . we can do something else . . . a distraction!'

'You mean pretend we're a regiment of lancers?' It was Emilio's sick joke.

'No, we can start a fire . . . I got the materials, and boy this is dry grass. Let's get to work.' He took out a cigar and then his tinderbox. He took a match and lit the cigar, then dismounted, shook out his little store of tinder and lit it. They were only 100 yards from where the boats had moored. 'Get flapping . . . we need a breeze, Emilio!'

The bank had seen no rain for a month, and the grass was bone dry. In minutes there was a sizable fire, and the billows of smoke in the dawn caught the eyes of the Mexicans. Emilio and John made for cover over the rise of the slope and rode along to be positioned behind the Mexicans, who had moved fast after seeing the drifting smoke.

'You're a genius, John Four Tongues!' Emilio called out.

'Yeah . . . and a dead one if you don't shut up!'

They heard orders being barked out down by the shore, and meantime the blaze grew and grew.

From where the Speke party had reached, they couldn't see the smoke. They had covered the track around a bend in the river and rested as dawn broke, sitting around the gravel spit that reached into the water. It was at that moment that Bernie Speke realized where they were, and he said, 'Now see . . . I been to this place afore . . . this here creek bends down to Laredo . . . a longer way in, but they might think we went on following the river. I say we track along the creek.'

'Fine. You all set off,' Jack said, 'Wate and me, we'll keep the Mexies busy . . . give you time.'

They looked back, expecting the pursuers to appear, but it was all still and quiet. Then, across the bank, two riders shouted out. They had been seen by

Emilio and John.

Liza jumped to her feet and called out Emilio's name. Her heart jumped with the joy of knowing he was alive, and so close. The two men rode on, saying they were looking for a ford where the horses could cross.

'You got some time . . . we delayed them . . . get moving!' Emilio called out.

The party wasted no time. Speke and Liza led, with the stretcher-carriers following and then the other men and women. It was slow progress, and though they were all tired, they found the strength to carry on, turning in towards the bank of the creek. It was now light and they had renewed hope. 'Daughter, the Good Lord has brought your man back to you . . . I'd given him up!' Bernie said.

Liza felt a weight lift from her, to think that Emilio was soon to be with them.

Back at the riverside, Jack and Wate sat, rifles at the ready. Time had moved on and still there was no sign of either the Mexicans or of the two riders across the water.

Wate, now chewing tobacco to pass the time, spat some out and said, 'Hell, can I just say again, the woman who's responsible for all this confusion in my life . . . well, was she worth it? I mean look at me now! I'm a loner, I know that. I come lookin' for you because I owed Jesse Carey after he saved my life in the Gold Nugget. I tracked you across all kinds of fiendish places, packed with trigger-happy madmen and wild Mexies, and for what? To end up sittin' here, waitin' to face an army of Mexican soldiers and to be mixed up in a battle . . . a damned great war, mister!'

'You're like me, Wate. You're an idealist. I'm here to prove I can do something good for once. You're here because you had the honour to pay back a man you owed. You could run. I mean, you could run now! Go on. . . .'

'Run, now? You crazy? The last few days have been the maddest, meanest, most dangerous ones I ever faced, and I been in some tricky old corners, back to the wall, Brady, let me tell you. This is a war! There are armies swarming all over this border. There could be the mother of all battles behind us in Laredo, and here I am, with a celebrated gunman, waiting to die. Me and the gunman against a regiment of Mexies. I think they're digging our graves right now, mister.'

'Well we're not completely alone . . . here come the riders.'

Sure enough, Emilio and John Four Tongues had made it across and they were now riding up. Soon they were shaking hands with Jack and Wate.

'Ah, I'll be dyin' with three other fools then!' Wate said, pretending to find the situation amusing.

'Don't mind him,' Jack said. 'Now, Emilio . . . Liza is that-a-way . . . they went along the creek there, a long route to the town. You gonna follow them?'

'I can't leave you here to fight . . . we made a distraction, but soon they'll be on the boats and comin' along here. I reckon there's around a hundred and thirty of them,' Emilio said. 'Thanks to John here, with some scout wisdom, we made it this far.'

This was troubling Jack Brady. More than anything in the world, he wanted to see Liza Speke happy. She would not be happy if her future husband was shot down in the river mud.

'John,' he asked, 'You got a woman? A wife?'

'No. I lost her to a fever.'

'Wate . . . you're a loner like me.' Jack looked around and seemed to think hard on something, screwing up his forehead. 'Way I see it, Emilio, you have to get along there, be the rearguard of Speke's crowd. We three fight here. You take the horses. You could ride ahead . . . get to Laredo first.'

He had just said those words when there was the sound of oars on the water, very close, and voices rapped out commands.

'You hear me, Texas Ranger?' Jack asked.

'I hear you, but a Ranger does not run away!'

'A Ranger with commitments . . . and a future . . . he does!' Jack said, and nodded towards the creek. 'Anyway, you ain't running away . . . you're the next barrel they face.'

Emilio did not want to turn and run, in any circumstances. It was ingrained in him to stand and fight. 'See, Brady, you don't know the Rangers. We don't expect to last long. We ride into the mouth of death and to hell with it all.'

'Well excuse me for being a killjoy, but fact is, if

116

you asked a woman for her hand, then you got to give her a future ... the one she's said she'll share with you ... I know that because I see my pa let a marriage slip away ... Let fools like us stay and fight.'

'Fine ... but don't do anything dumb, like get killed, you hear?' he said and then ran off, shouting 'The Lone Star Forever!'

12

'Like I was sayin' just before you came, Mister Tonkawa, how I came to be in this fight, I do not know. How did you?'

'I'm a soldier for the States. The Mounted Rifles are my outfit. They're my family, Mister Wate.'

'You sure are lucky. I could use a mighty large family right now, all armed to the teeth.'

'Speaking of which,' Jack asked, 'What do we have . . . a rifle each, and maybe a revolver?'

They both nodded. Jack looked around. He was searching for the best position. He was wishing he still had his Appaloosa with him, and Evan Wate was feeling the same. 'Look, our job here is simple. We hold them for as long as possible. The longer we do that, the more chance there is of the Spekes surviving and reaching Laredo. It's not far at all. Another hour, they could be there, according to Bernie.'

They nodded and seemed to see the point. Jack kept looking, and then he saw the best place to be.

'You two . . . see that ledge up there? It's got some green cover. We need to be there. It's got rocks too . . . a line that will make for a perfect little shooting nest. We'll look down on 'em. They'll be scared of us.'

'Sure . . . so scared. Three against a hundred and more. Very sensible, Brady . . . come on then.' Wate was still in his usual mood of dark humour.

They scrambled to the ledge and sat in half-cover. Just as they were settled, the first sounds of the Mexicans could be heard, and from where they were, they saw just one boat hitting the shore and men started to jump out. 'I see Herrera,' John said, 'I know him well . . . fought him many times.'

'What kind of a man is he?' Wate asked.

'He is a man without a soul. Dead in the eyes. You can see that . . . they say he has murdered women and children. His time will come. . . .'

Jack was counting. 'Now look . . . he's sent just one boat. Herrera has come with only some . . . I'm counting thirty men.'

'Oh that's fine then . . . odds of ten to one!' Wate laughed.

'Now, me and you, John, we got Hall carbines, and we have Patersons. We can put a lot of lead their way pretty quick. What you got, Wate? Ah you got the Paterson revolver . . . and that damned long knife. Well I guess you won't get close enough to use that.'

Jack was working things out. He could see that their one advantage was surprise, and that the path from the shore was narrow, along the foot of the ridge. This meant that the Mexicans would maybe come in twos. One rapid round of fire at the first half dozen men would buy some time. Herrera would have to think a while, or keep sending more men to die.

In Laredo the Texan and States forces were assembling. It was a question of waiting for the Mexican army to arrive. The Mexicans had taken the town and lost it, and it was a sure bet that they were setting out to grab it back now. Gillespie and the other officers were ordered to dig in on the western outskirts and wait for the attack. They occupied every defensible corner they could find, and were half a mile out of the town, knowing that a charge would be the key manoeuvre in the defence. Gillespie and McCulloch, leading the Rangers and the Volunteers, were given the task of leading a charge from the position outside the town, and they were now in place, expecting trouble any time soon.

Pastor Jim was eating away at his nerves, he was worrying so much. He had no notion of where Brady might be, nor Emilio, and as for Liza, well, he had promised his friend to watch out for her and keep her safe, and now here he was, pacing along a line of rocks, heaps of sand, piled shrubs and dead wood, unable to do anything but pray. He thought of asking Gillespie to send men out to scout around up river, but that was asking too much. He fixed his stare on the horizon, and longed for the sight of horses, or even folk on feet – anything to suggest that there might be life out there.

Gillespie searched him out. They had been friends for a few years, and the Ranger captain knew exactly what Jim was thinking.

'You got someone out there . . . someone close. Who is it?'

'It's the Speke family . . . and Brady, who I got out of jail!'

'Oh, well I must say, some of my best fighters for Texas are men who stepped over from the wrong side of the law, Jim, old friend. As to Speke, I've heard about the man. Tough as buffalo hide, I heard. The kind of man we could use in the Rangers, but he went his own way.'

'Yes, Jack Brady goes his own way as well, and it's usually the path to hell!'

Gillespie thought for a minute, then spoke in measured tones, with a deep frown on his weathered face. 'Pastor, we need your Man in Heaven I think. We need him right now. Think you could say a word on my behalf?'

'I'll try.'

'The point is, Laredo is the sort of spot that the Mexies want. Just in the right place for holding any outfit coming down from the border. We need to keep it.'

'I know how you Texans work . . . you don't give much credence to standing still.'

121

Gillespie scanned the distance one more time, then said, 'You heard right. We hit 'em hard while they're deliberatin' then ask questions later when we're roundin' up prisoners . . . if there are any!'

'Wait . . . see. . . .' Jim pointed to the north. 'There . . . to the east of the river . . . is that a road?'

'It's a creek. What do you see?'

'People . . . maybe a horse . . . I think they're walking! Surely not.'

On the creek bank, Bernie Speke was looking their way, and he felt a welcome sense of triumph and hope as he knew he was almost at Laredo.

Jack, Wate and John Four Tongues were ready, fingers on triggers, eyes concentrated on the edge of the river between the rockface and the water. Jack felt the trail of sweat run from his forehead down across an eyelid, and he sensed his heartbeat thudding up in his throat. Then there were voices, followed by the sight of four or five men in a group, all wearing broad hats, capes and light jackets. One had a lance.

'Now!' Jack snapped out, and all three rifles sent bullets into the advancing soldiers. 'They're Herrera's men! Come on, four down! Now pistols!' Jack shouted. The three fired again, and men following the first Mexicans were too late to run. Three more came down.

There was a moment of quiet except for the voice of an officer shouting his commands. 'Typical of the

Mexican army to send in the *comancheros* and irregulars . . . the fancy blue jackets will be way behind!' John said.

They were ready with the rifles again, but this time several lines of men appeared and sprinted towards them, then ducked under cover. These men were armed and they fired up towards the ledge. But they were vulnerable. Some were picked off, but their fire was relentless. Jack could see that their intensive fire was to keep the three holed in. 'They're sending men behind . . .' he called out, over the noise of gunfire. 'There's a plateau above us . . . some will come that way and come down behind us!'

Wate and John cowered low for cover. They could only nod, agreeing with Jack. It was a risk, but it had to be done: Jack would run up the short slope to their left, to the plateau, and wait for the Mexicans behind.

There were lulls in the fire from below, and in the pauses, other soldiers ran behind and into the shore area beneath. Some few were now blue-jackets, men from Silveras's battalion. John and Wate kept up their fire, but they were open to more accurate shots when they reloaded. There was movement below, and Wate said, 'John . . . they're running in below, out of sight. They're gonna climb up.'

Meanwhile, Jack was lying in some cover, and sure enough, three men came into sight only ten yards away, after climbing up on the easy slope side. He took careful aim with his rifle, and one went down.

The others had pistols and swords and ran at him. His Paterson rapped out death to the nearest one, and then Jack swung the gun around as the man closed in with his sword, swinging brutally towards Jack's face. He ducked, and lunged for the man's feet. Then they were both down in the dust, and all weapons were abandoned. It was now a matter of hands, fists, determination. The Mexican was small but strong, and his tough hands went for Jack's throat. At first, it was a struggle for breath, and Jack thought he was done for; but from somewhere deep down he found the strength to push an arm up and break the stranglehold. The man was pushed back and sprawled in the dirt. As he staggered to his feet, and his sabre had been lost from his grip, he snatched a dagger from his belt and came at Jack, who forced himself to fix all his attention on the blade, and on the man's wrist. As the attacker's arm swung at him, Jack went for it and gripped it hard. He hauled the assailant down beneath him, and the man squirmed in the dust, losing the grip on the dagger.

From the corner of an eye, Jack saw another soldier arriving at the top of the bluff. He had just seconds to drop the man beneath. One punch to the side of the head put him unconscious, and then some instinct in Jack, coming from a dozen fights in cow-towns and dead-end bars, made him roll to one side, as the new attacker's sword blade stuck in the dirt and shivered.

Jack turned around, got to his feet, and gave the man a blow to the back of his neck. As he fell, Jack was on him, wrenching back his head until a crack of bone told him that the man was dead.

Now John and Wate appeared from the other side. They had run from their position. 'They're climbing . . . too many of 'em, Jack. We have to run for more cover!' John cried out.

'There . . . see that dip . . . we lie in that, so we see their advance from the dirt. They won't see all of us!' John said. He had survived plenty of deadly engagements with *comancheros* in his scouting life. It was *comancheros* who now ran at them, as all three lay flat to the earth, rifles reloaded. The attackers were a rough-looking lot, a mix of fighting jackets and breeches, some being part-Indian and others Mexican. Some of them wore United States cavalry hats and coats; others had dirty, torn Mexican coats and hats. One wore a dark blue shako.

'They are the scum of the border riders . . . Herrera's men. . . .' John said. 'Fire . . . now!'

Their shots stopped the attack. Three of the six men fell. The others ran back to hide where they could. Then, after the smoke cleared and every man involved seemed to pause and look around, a voice rang out from somewhere behind the rocks near the far slope. 'This is Captain Koni Herrera speaking. It is time to give yourselves up. Put your hands up, walk out into the light, and you will be spared.'

'Sure, and my pa is president of the United

States!' Evan Wate returned, managing a laugh.

'I give you my word as an officer of Mexico, and an aristocrat,' Herrera replied.

'I give you my bullet,' Wate said, firing at the spot where the voice came from.

There was another silence. It gave Jack time to speak. 'Look, I guess we've taken enough of them out to worry Herrera. We just stay put.'

Herrera called out again, this time with a restlessness in his tone. 'Look, gentlemen, if you are saying no to me, then one option is open to you . . . to say your prayers!'

'Listen up, *Capitan*. . . . You're speaking to a Ranger, a soldier and a big man who hates to be bullied . . . you want some more corpses to drag home, just keep on doing what you're doing. I'm Jack Brady, and you're starting to annoy me.'

There was a laugh from Herrera, but it was the kind of laugh you might hear at a funeral when somebody told a tale of the deceased's violent end. '*Muy buen* . . . then so be it. You have five minutes, so I can see to my wounded.'

The three men in the dirt, rifles held ready, knew that the next rush at them would be aimed at engulfing them. Sheer weight of numbers was Herrera's best tactic now, and they knew it.

'Load up, put your pistols by your side, and your knives in your teeth. . . .' Jack said. 'We don't go down easy.'

The little dip in the contours of the shoreline was

to their advantage, and John knew this better than the others. As a scout, his first thought was always one of cover, disguise, being unseen. He whispered a reassurance to his comrades. He told them that the dip before them gave a foot drop, lowering them from sight. They had found a small haven of protection, by accident.

'We lay the guns and knives ready,' Jack said, 'We take them in turn. In a second between each one, we can give rapid fire and strong defence here, as they have to run for twenty yards before they reach us.' He had come to see that the Mexicans never troubled to make a line or use ranks of rifle fire. It was all a rush and a scream with them. As he lay there, studying the terrain, he saw that the action of wind and water over the centuries had worn the shoreline heights and creeks into a succession of natural dens, for hunted animals or for desperate men – as they were now. It was a game of patience. If they could stay still for hours, like a hunted rat with a predator circling above him, then they would have the advantage when the daylight came. Herrera was not going to dig in and wait. He had the numerical advantage. But his haste would be his undoing – if they stayed firm and still.

It was a case of encouragement and support through that long night. Jack had in his pocket some small chunks of hardtack. His instinct had made him tuck them away, with some tough biscuit. He fed the other two small bits, at intervals. Far worse for them was the lack of water. Yet they were inured to such deprivation. John Four Tongues, Jack concluded, must have learned to survive on damp air and hope. He was lean, fine-limbed as a Comanche mustang, and alert as a hawk with a victim in sight.

John gave the best help. 'Let your mind go somewhere else,' he said, whispering. 'What you must learn, to go home alive, and not be carried to your grave pyre, is to be *away* . . . take the mind *away*. . . .'

They looked at him, puzzled. John went on, 'Away . . . not here. If the mind is not here, it cannot feel pain or it cannot let in the weak thoughts, the thoughts of a defeated one. You understand?'

They understood. Jack never thought that he would be feeling like a kid in a schoolroom in the middle of that desperate run for life, but he was, and from this Tonkawa he saw something stronger maybe than steel and lead. They might have been in the position of three hunted critters, but they could rise above the troubles weighing them down, and wait for the right moment to act.

Evan Wate, as always, made a contribution to lighten the load in another way. 'See,' he said, shifting the weight from his elbows to his side, lurching heavily to take some weight from an uncomfortable edge of his muscle, he said, 'Personally, I find that I lose my mind real easy like.'

'You're fixing to stay alive using all your wits and this here weaponry, Evan Wate, and you still make light of it all,' Jack said.

'Sure. I make light of it all because I never figured out how to carry anything heavy . . . you understand?'

'You would make a Tonkawa scout,' John said, 'You brush away the sadness. You are a man of the light.'

'Now remember,' Jack said, 'no sleep . . . no movement. Do anything you have to do right here . . . then we use these in turn . . . rifle, revolver, knife. . . .'

He was doing his best to appear confident. Inside, he was as lost as the others, and just as desperate. But life had taught him to put a front on, face everything out, and never show weakness. His most encouraging thought was that, when he thought of the enemy around that rock, in the grass, he knew that they would be thinking of how many friends they had lost. That would make them thirst for vengeance, of course, but it would also give them the sting of fear.

13

Bernie Speke was still sore and in pain, but he was able to do what he always did – lead and show the way. He might have lost his beloved Fortress but he still had his life, and his daughter, and now he even had his future son-in-law. He knew that too many rests and pauses would put them all in danger, but he also knew that pushing and driving them on with too much vigour would bring some to their knees with exhaustion. His reasoning was that the men who stayed behind would stall the Mexicans for maybe an hour or two, but no longer, and when they came after them, they would be very fast. Still, he had two men with rifles walking at the rear, and what was most heartening was the fact that Laredo was coming closer and closer with every stride.

It took some considerable time for Liza and Emilio to spend any time apart after he joined the Speke party plodding along the creek to Laredo. The young man took the news of Bill Cheto's death real bad. It was like he had lost his best friend – a sort of father and brother in one, and he felt this because they had always had a special bond, riding out like partners, and Emilio learning how to survive in the wild places their lives took them to. That loss brought them closer, as Liza saw how much reassurance and comfort her man needed. They had been too long apart, and now there was still fear and uncertainty in the air around them. Every minute of the journey was nervous; they were all jumpy as new foals let loose on the grass. When Emilio told the Spekes what Jack Brady had done, they stood in amazement, as the walkers rested for a minute, to give the stretcher-carriers a rest. The story was told with a feeling of deep respect.

'Mr Speke . . . they won't come back. That Brady man . . . he's given his life for us . . . for Texas leastways.'

'Who is that man?' Speke asked nobody in particular. 'I mean he turns up, with that tall fella, and they act like some kind of fighters from the Lord . . . I mean, are they tired of livin' or somethin'?'

'Whoever he is, I wish we had a regiment of 'em,' Emilio said.

There were only nods of agreement and mutterings of thanks and amazement, all agreeing with Speke's summing up.

'Emilio,' Liza said quietly, thinking of Jack's face the last time they spoke, 'Emilio, Brady has saved us. You and me, I mean. He's just a man we met in

131

Callego, right? He was a stranger there . . . just blown in by the wind. Do we think he's really saved us?'

'Not yet . . . but he's given us a fighting chance.' Emilio said, looking back into the unknown behind them. 'He's given us time . . . I'd say he knew there was enough time for us to outrun the Mexicans. The problem is . . . I have to say, I don't give much for his chances of reaching Laredo . . . I reckon they were outgunned back there!'

They looked at each other, and Emilio's look searched her face for the smallest trace of meaning, some clue as to what she was dealing with, deep inside. He would never know what she felt, what images came to her mind as she thought of Jack Brady standing against a battalion . . . for her. Who was that man? She had had plenty of time to think about him as the party trudged southwards, gradually heading for safety. What had made him do such a thing? What and who was he? He had come from nowhere and done something truly remarkable, along with the tall man and the Tonkawa. The scout she saw as a soldier of the States; but Jack and the tall one, they had ridden into her life from some mysterious place, and for some mysterious reason.

But one thing she felt, and felt deeply: Jack had felt something special for her. His look had said it, better than words. Now his actions were saying it, and a man could do no more than put his life on the line.

Captain Gillespie fired questions at Speke and his

party, as Liza took the injured to a sick-house in the town. The defenders wanted to know who was fighting with Mexico, and what was happening along the Rio Grande. Though exhausted, every man was questioned; then Gillespie and Speke had some time to decide on what and who might be coming towards Laredo. Bernie Speke was glad to down a few whiskies and have a doctor look at his wound. Brady had done well: the man was gaining a rare reputation now around the Rangers' temporary home on the fringe of Laredo.

'Captain Gillespie,' said Bernie, 'the information appears to be that a considerable force . . . a regiment . . . is mixed with the border detachments, the scum, in my words . . . and they're joining General Arista. He's smartin' from Resaca and Palo Alto. His attack on us here will be desperation. I think, a matter of honour, do you agree?'

'Oh sure . . . he's certain to be replaced if I know anything about the Mexicans. But whatever he sends at us, you must know that we'll charge 'em. Coffee Hays has no other way of fightin.' He paused to think before adding, 'Course, I expect you and your party to rest up. You've earned some time away from warfare. While I'm on the subject, your Fortress . . . how did it fall? Any cannon?'

'Sheer numbers. No cannon . . . just too many men came at us and the river was our saviour, Sir. Now it's Jack Brady as well, and he ain't even a Texan!'

Gillespie's Rangers and Volunteers dug in, but that was just to have a line for supporting fighters to occupy. They were preparing to charge, to ride at full tilt at whatever army came across the plain to the east. It was the only way that Hays and the new Texan fighters could work. While they made ready, checking and rechecking their weapons and horses, Bernie Speke looked to the north, up the river, and his daughter, resting from her nursing of the sick and wounded, lay in Emilio's arms and thought of Jack Brady, and where he might be.

There was one man, though, who was too restless to sit and wait. Parson Jim was not going to leave his young friend to his fate. He now knew that Emilio was safe, and he knew that Eliza was safe. Bullhead would be happy if he knew, and soon he would be told, God willing. But Pastor Jim had an intuition, and he believed in his intuition. The voice inside him told him to ride up river and find his friend Jack Brady. At times of rare emergency, he argued, a man of God had to shoulder a gun and be a Christian soldier. Maybe, he told himself, a bunch of Mexicans out to take lives and inflict suffering deserved a quick exit to hell. Maybe what could do that was a stick or two of dynamite.

His talk with Gillespie shocked the old soldier. Here was a padre asking for dynamite. 'You're going on your own, Jim?' He asked.

'I'd like to have some of your best explosive

packed in my saddle-bag please, in case certain individuals will not listen to the word of God.'

'You're crazed, deranged. Anyway, priests do not take lives!'

'I'll take my collar off when I do it.'

'You'll go without my blessing, Pastor Jim.'

But go he did. He set out late that night, following the creek, where Speke told him he would need to travel to reach Jack. He followed the water, at a steady gallop, talking himself into the unsafe belief that sometimes you took a life to save a life.

On the ground on the high ground above the Rio Grande, Jack, Wate and John Four Tongues were ready for the next attack. Night was closing in. Would Herrera come in the dark, sending the whole force against them? Jack knew that such a move was the only way to root out three desperate men who were holed up in dirt and shadow.

'Jack Brady, I ask you again, how come I'm here? I mean, I was after you for seducing the woman, and look what happened to me? I become a fighter for a place I never been to and I never knowed! What kind of black magic do you use on a man? I mean, chances are this set of bandits are gonna ravage the place and run through us like a herd of buffalo, and here I am just waitin' for 'em. Can you explain that?'

'I can explain it, Evan Wate. You know I'm innocent of the charge. You know it was a man who looked like me. Ever since I was a kid, my neighbour Square John was took for being me. It's well-known around Wellport County . . . you ask anybody!'

'Well I would, but I'll be food for flies by tomorrow. What a way to end it all! I thought that my last day was meant to be as a newspaper man. I always wanted to run a paper.'

'You will, Evan Wate . . . I promise you. When we've crushed these Mexies, we'll get back to somewhere east and peaceful, and I'll buy you a newspaper. Promise.'

John was amused at all this. Their way of talking was something he would never do, and the humour was lost on him. All he could tell was that these men were mad. They were loco. There was no other explanation. Consequently he decided to add his own words. 'For me, my friends, I always wanted to be a soldier . . . wanted to fight Comanches, the enemies of my people. But no, the gods frowned on me and here I am fighting against impossible odds . . . Worse, I'm fighting with two men who hate each other!'

'Not so impossible,' Jack said. 'They have lost maybe half of the force they came with. My maths tells me there's fifteen of them out there, with Herrera himself.'

'Five to one . . . sounds manageable . . . if you say it real quick,' Wate said.

Jack knew that their real enemy now was sleep. He made it clear to the others that they had to fight sleep. Herrera would rush at them if he sensed that they were not on edge and ready to fight. As night encroached, they watched each other. At the slightest nod of the head, of any one of them, the others would shake them awake again. Every rustle in the undergrowth startled them into alertness, with their fingers hovering on the triggers of the rifles. Every little animal squeak set their hearts beating too fast, and even a snake slithering around behind them turned their heads.

Finally, dawn came and there had been no move from Herrera. Jack knew that he was playing with their fears. Waiting and silence breed fear. A hunted man expects the worst after every quiet second. But the Mexicans were stirring; there were sounds to verify that, and the three men, still lying in the dust, tightened their grip on their weapons.

'Remember . . . when they come, pick your man, take a second or two, choose the target well . . . and then pick up the revolver, as they come closer. Hopefully, they won't fire as they run.' Jack said all this with his nose almost in the earth. There was not too much height of cover there for them.

Suddenly, there was a chorus of screams and yells, as a line of men appeared in front, racing at them, with pistols pointed and blasting. A bullet slammed into John Four Tongues, hitting his forehead, and he went down with a yelp as the shock went through him.

But two Mexicans went down from the rifle fire, and in a split second, Jack and Wate were firing their Patersons, strafing the front line. Men went down with screams of pain. Others, behind, turned and ran. Then there was silence again until the familiar voice of Herrera called, 'That was not a clever thing to do. Now you must look behind you!'

There was a cut into the silence, as a knife stuck into the cottonwood by Wate's head. They turned, to see three men behind, raising their rifles to fire. Jack and Wate rolled sideways and the bullets missed them.

'Run higher!' Jack called, and they both went for the cover of the rock-side. There was another fifteen feet of rock that they could run up, and there they could find a position on higher ground. As they ran, slugs shot past, so close they felt the breeze.

Jack thanked fate when he saw the thin defile ahead, between the highest part of the bluff. It was a slice in between, the width of two men, and they took it, running into the gulley and then turning to face whatever followed.

'They have to be almost all wiped out, Wate. You been countin' them?'

'No, but I've had enough. I say we rush 'em. Come on!' There was no thought involved. Instinct told them that to be holed up in such a confined space was asking for an unpleasant death. They were vulnerable there, to anything hurled in at them. Out they rushed, throwing away any cautious thought, just firing their revolvers ahead. Someone squealed and there was a body in the dust. They froze and looked at a line of men in front of them. But before anything was done or said, there was a voice from somewhere to their left, and heads turned. There was Pastor Jim, and he shouted, 'Get back in cover, Jack!' Then he threw a stick towards the Mexican line.

Gunfire blasted at the same time, as once again, Jack and Wate dived for the earth and rolled to one side, covering their heads as an almighty crack of sound went above them. There was an acrid smell, drifting smoke, and some cries of pain. Jack and Wate finally stood up as it all cleared, and before them were six bodies, including that of Herrera, and another man lay dead around fifty yards away. It was Pastor Jim.

14

Jack ran to Pastor Jim, fast as he could, and bent over him to check if he was breathing. He had been hit in the chest and the leg and was bleeding so much and so fast that they both knew nothing could be done. Jack held his friend's head up a little from the dust. There were signs of life – just. 'Padre . . . padre, listen . . . you'll be fine. Just keep still and. . . .'

'I will not be fine, Jack Brady. What kept you so long? Look, please tell my friend Bullhead I never got a chance to watch out for his Emilio or Liza . . . I was always too far away . . . tell him they're good, that they live. Promise? My friend Bullhead, he thought of Emilio as a son and as his best friend. Promise you'll tell him.'

'I do. Padre . . . I have to tell you thanks for what you did for me. . . .'

'I took life, Jack. I took life. A man shouldn't juggle with friends and enemies. I failed.'

'No, no . . . you're a good man . . . a good man.'

Jack saw the padre fade out of life and into silence. His body fell limp.

There were two graves to make. When it came to John Four Tongues, Jack and Wate had no knowledge of the Tonkawa to share, and so there was no notion as to how they should lay him to rest or what to say over his body. The first heap of stones, over John, then, were laid with a mix of words and thoughts all related to what general beliefs were held by the Indians, and here Jack's experience led him to say no more than that they were saying farewell to a brave man. 'He walked with us, and he fought by us, and he gave his life to help keep us alive. You can't ask no more than that, Wate.'

'No, Brady. This time you're talking sense. You don't always do that, but this time you are.'

'That you saying something complimentary, Evan Wate?'

'I wouldn't say that. Just that you did well enough and you spoke truth.'

Burying Pastor Jim was the toughest thing that Jack Brady had ever done. He struggled to find some words to say once the two men stood over the heap of stones they had piled over the body. Jack searched his mind for religious words but none were found. Eventually, as they looked nervously at each other, Jack said, 'This man lying here turned my life around. I met him in the middle of nowhere and he changed me by saying almost nothing. He's got to be the best preacher in the world, and I can only hope that you will forgive him, Lord, for taking the lives of those Mexicans. That's not exactly what a padre is supposed to do. But here lies a truly good man, who did, like Christ himself, die for others. Is that going too far, Wate, do you think?'

'I reckon it is. I mean Jesus was real special, right?'

'This man Jim was real special. But then, I never did believe in any sermons and stuff until this man came along. May he rest in peace then.'

Wate said the same and both men found whatever plant was near that had any bloom about it, and these were thrown on the stones.

The walk back was exhausting. Both men were so used to riding, and they sorely missed their horses. But it was a case of following the creek south. After a few hours of daylight and nothing to eat, Jack stuck out a hand and pointed across towards the fringes of Laredo. 'See . . . all that dust . . . hundreds of riders! Must be the Mexicans.'

'We're too late for the battle . . . it's all built up and there's hell to come!' Wate said.

'No, we're pretty close. Come on.'

'Just a minute,' Wate said, 'I never yet ran to take a bullet, and I ain't startin' now.' He walked, with an even pace, though his strides were long. Jack had to smile at him, and stayed walking with him. They were inching nearer and nearer to an ever-growing Mexican cavalry line, although they didn't know it yet.

*

On the fringes of Laredo, Gillespie and McCulloch were filling their spot in the line of defence. The Mounted Rifles and other States cavalry extended over half a mile, and to their west, the Rangers and Volunteers, stood by to mount and do what they always did – go straight for the throat of the enemy.

Speke and his party, including Liza, were keeping close to the sick and wounded, a way back behind, but Emilio and Tammy had joined the Rangers.

'Now,' Gillespie said, from the saddle, addressing the ranks of his men, now all mounted, and staring out at the dust on the horizon, 'Now this is the real thing . . . an actual fight! Rangers and Volunteers . . . this is the moment you trained for. The enemy are there now, and they all want to kill you and ride through you to take this town. You got that? Now, Texans defend by charging! We're going to run at them, screaming and firing. Remember the Comanche way . . . the best horsemen in the world I guess. We learned from them folk. We learned that a gutful of courage and line of men bringing death tends to break an enemy. These Mexicans, they're still stuck in the way wars were fought years back.'

The line was raggle-taggle: some in the grey jackets and blue breeches of the Rangers as they should be, ideally, but most in any kind of attire they could lay their hands on. The horses were nervy, trying to swing around, but the riders were bossing the day, and the lines were ready to go as a voice from the top of an adobe stable building shouted:

'Here they come!'

The Texans could see the line of blue. There were maybe four hundred cavalry coming at them. But the Mexicans expected a defensive ploy, with men dug in or well covered behind obstacles. What they got was a blood-curdling charge. The Mexicans jabbed sabres forward, as cavalry had done in Napoleon's wars; the officers bawled out commands. They were met by men swinging low on their mounts, firing from the side, low down, where they were not targets; they were met by men and horses at full gallop, with rifles blazing, and then, with the rifles slipped into leather, there were revolvers firing at them.

General Arista looked on, seeing Silveras's men and the other two battalions allotted to the west of the line of attack, crumbling and running for their lives. The attack dispersed, and horses ran wildly in all directions. Some followed the river and some the creek or the plain. Their riders had been toppled by rifle fire or the gunfire following; there was now hand-to-hand fighting as the battle progressed to a desperate stage for the Mexicans.

Jack and Wate, now close enough to see some of this combat, found that they had the gift of horses. They collared them as they drank from the creek, and soon they were digging in their heels and riding to Laredo. They rode through the melee in which men were struggling against each other, in a desperate lock of hands and arms; Commands were screamed out over the deafening sound of the battle. Mexican officers shouted for no retreat but their soldiers ran past them, sprinting away for their lives.

Along the line, the Mounted Rifles were doing their part, and Tammy was back with his regiment. The States troopers and cavalry were slower moving forward, but just as effective as the Texans. In all the chaos, Gillespie rode around to register where there might be trouble, where there could be any weakness. But it was clear that the day was his and, of course, his commander, Coffee Hays.

Gillespie saw Emilio in the thick of it, grappling hand-to-hand with a Mexican rider, and coming off the winner, warding off a knife thrust and knocking out the man with a swing of a rifle butt.

Running through the dense mass of bodies struggling to stay alive, Jack and Wate had to confront whatever faced them. In the confusion it was hard to distinguish who was friend or foe. All they knew for sure was that the Mexicans – some of them – wore shakos. But soon they realized that the States men sometimes wore high hats, and again it was almost impossible to tell who was who. One thing only could be relied upon – if a man stood before you and jabbed a blade at you, or swung a rifle, then you fought him. Riders at times galloped past, some dipping lances and some bending low to curl a deadly sabre blade towards a face. Jack raised an arm to fend off a blow, and gradually, his arms and hands

were sore and smarting with cuts and wounds. As for
Wate, a tall man was an easy target and he knew this.
His instinct led him to crouch and take a position he
could defend. He knew that his best hope was to
snatch a rifle and sit back, dealing with anyone who
came at him.

Jack and Wate were parted in the mess and chaos
of the fierce engagement; but as the hours wore on
and bit by bit, there were spaces between gaggles of
fighters where men had fallen. A little more light
came through after a few hours. Still the frenzy of
killing went on, with the shouts of officers behind,
accompanying every thrust and every turn from a
flash of steel.

Horses were brought down and men impaled;
bullets cracked into heads and bellies. Coats that
were blue or white at midday became sullied with
blood and grime. Men fought through heat and
sweat, finding strength where they thought it had all
ebbed away. Even the sound of drums and trumpets
communicated nothing that Jack or Wate could
interpret. A command to advance was no different
to them than a command to retreat.

Eventually, a rider streamed through the rabble
shouting, 'They're on the run ... they're on the
run!' The rider, Jack saw, was a States rifleman. It was
his first inkling that there was a victory, and it was the
one he longed for.

When the last desperate combat between fading
and weakening men fell away to nothing more than

grunts and cries of pain, Jack sat on the earth between a dead horse and a pile of bodies, and he looked around. It was all senseless, meaningless. What was all this killing being done for? His reasoning told him that it was all about putting a particular name on a piece of a map. It was about what existed at one side of a borderline and what was across it. Enemies could be allies the next day. The following day they could change again, and it all led to this – men squealing in pain, some looking at the end of everything and some just so dry and hollowed out that they were next door to death, and they knew it.

But he was sitting there, alive. He had survived. He felt his arm, pinching it to be sure that he had sensation. Yes, he was alive. He was not a ghost walking the field of the dead. He kept on poking, searching for anything familiar. The corpses all looked the same. The uniforms appeared to melt away into one murky colour, reinforcing the idea of death as the great leveller. Yet, finally, as two or three men staggered around looking lost and weak, there was the unmistakeable frame of Evan Wate. The tall, thin man smiled as he saw Jack and called out, 'Jack Brady . . . you're still here! So am I. . . .'

Jack stood up and they shook hands, each feeling the caked sweat on the other's skin. 'Does this mean we're soldiers, Jack Brady? Because I never asked to be one!'

'Reckon it would be tough to say we were not . . . we're all torn up . . . see my ripped coat? A battle is all about being torn to shreds and getting hot as a furnace. Shall we find a drink, Mister Wate?'

That sounded like a good idea to Wate: his thirst was huge. He felt he could drink a river. Then, together, treading as slow as an old-timer or a stubborn mule going up a mountain, they went, step after exhausted step, out from the stench and the smoke and towards whatever might be waiting back where the trumpet had been heard. 'I guess any generals around will be back there, sipping whiskey . . . not here biting lead!' Wate said, still finding a joke in him underneath the pain.

'You ever thought about going on the stage, Mr Wate?' Jack asked, as they plodded on.

'Only to scrub and clean it, I guess. My ma always said I was a good liar, and that's the same as an actor, ain't it?' He chuckled and then held a painful spot on his side. 'Hell, I think I was cut here . . . only a nick. I was a nick away from nothing!'

They walked on, and inch by inch, the air around them began to clear. The cries and moans faded into the distance. Both looked ahead, their minds fixed on anything familiar, any face they might know. Where they had pains and bleeding, the agony subsided the nearer they came to somewhere clear of the fight. Their wounds stung and smarted; they felt the aching in every joint that had been used as the last dregs of strength were called upon when the enemy flailed blades at them and flung death at them in a hundred different ways.

*

As the intensity of the fight subsided, Speke and Liza walked out to join other medics in attending to the wounded. In the foul smoke blowing over the land, Liza, giving water to a man suffering from shock, staggering about the field of battle, shocked and numbed by the confusion and noise, looked up to see Jack Brady. They wrapped their arms around each other, Liza sobbing with the massive relief of seeing him alive.

'You made it, Liza . . . you made it . . . and Emilio?' Jack asked.

'He's out there fighting still,' she said.

'Jack Brady . . . there's one thing to say, and it's all that matters,' Liza said. 'You saved our lives. I never thought I would see you again and. . . .' She was fighting back tears. Jack put a finger to her lips and said, 'Nothing more for you to say, Liza. You and me, well we shared something good . . . good feelings I guess, and that's more than rare, so I thank you. Now we pray that your man rides back here.'

Jack joined the remnants of the Rangers who had stayed close to the defence line. The day was won for Gillespie and for the States army, too, with Zachary Taylor in command. As the day wore on and the last small-scale confrontations took place, the Mexicans began to withdraw. Someone reported that Silveras had retreated and was nowhere to be seen. All eyes were on who was moving around about 500 yards ahead, where there was a cloud of dust and now very little heard in terms of voices or commands. This meant that standing at the defence line, Speke, Liza, Jack and Wate stood and waited, their eyes fixed on that dirt cloud. Shapes rode or walked out of it, one by one. Eyes searched features, clothes and walks, for anything familiar – something that would tell them who was coming back alive and well.

Time went on, and their hearts beat more strongly than ever with the possibility of what and who could be lost forever. But then, after three hours, Emilio came walking slowly out. He was limping and he was holding a wound in his arm. Liza ran to him, and others helped him back. He was alive.

It took Evan Wate to remind Jack of something that had most likely slipped from his mind, as there were plenty of matters to chew over and understand. They were exhausted, and sat on barrels, coughing and clearing their lungs, when Wate paused, looked Jack in the eye and said, 'You do know that you're riskin' a death sentence, don't you, Brady?'

'Death sentence? What have I done?'

'Oh Brady, come on! You are a member of the Texas Volunteers. You signed up for six months, remember?'

These words were like a dark cloud passing over a sunny lawn in Jack's mind. He had given no thought to that during all the whirlwind of shooting and killing that had happened around him.

'Wate . . . I could run for it. Ain't nobody likely to

150

chase me across the borders and back up to Kansas, which is where I aim to be. Can we cut out now . . . after some mighty quick goodbyes?'

'Come on, saddle up the Mexican horses. Grab some food and pick up a rifle while there's a number lying around. It's not stealin' as we earned it. Plunder of war, don't they call it?' Wate liked the idea the more he talked about it.

'Yeah . . . *booty*. I hate the word. Let's go.'

I've done more than enough for Texas and for the United States, Jack thought. If there had been any kind of debt hanging over him, then now it was paid in full. His life had been out there in the open, for the taking, and all for a cause different from the cause he had always fought for – that of Jack Brady.

'What you have to tell yourself, Brady, is that you don't even belong here. You were just passin' through. I mean my case is different. I was trapped like a cat in a net, and mostly that was down to you. But you . . . well you got so much shame in you that you're a real easy man to persuade.'

'Shame?'

'Yeah . . . you got somethin' to prove. I seen a heap o' men like you down the years. They got somethin' to prove. They feel they fell short somehow, back in time. That you?'

Jack was thinking that the tall man was not as slow and one-sided as he looked. He was a thinker.

'I done my part then, Wate. Come on. There's a track out there, waiting for us.'

151

Jack spoke that way, but inside there was still the haunting thought that he had signed up to be a soldier and was now changing his mind. But surely, he told himself, he had packed in more than six months of soldiering in that battle at Laredo? He knew what Pa would say. He would argue that there's no measuring goodness and the right thing. 'Dammit . . . I done the right thing, Pa!' He said this well above a whisper, and Wate heard him.

'There you go, Brady . . . shame! I told you.'

It was all done as stealthy as a midnight thief might work. Whispers of farewell were given to Bernie Speke and to Emilio, who had to approve in spite of regulations. He swore to keep silent about them. If asked, he would say that Volunteer J. Brady had died in battle.

Then there were handshakes, the gathering of supplies into packs and wallets, and after an exchange of looks and smiles between Jack and Liza, the two men rode out north, taking a roundabout way towards the coast, aiming to ride up following the coast tracks.

He was thinking how he would most likely never see Liza again. But life had taught him that where you have a tie of emotions, and it can't work out, the best thing was to grit your teeth and cut the strings loose. Saying goodbye and riding out was worse than anything in the fight he had just survived. He knew that he would have her lodged in his mind for all his days to come.

Before he left, she had come to him to shake his hand, as all the Speke party shook his hand, but Liza leaned to speak softly in his ear. 'Jack, when you left us back there at the creek, and we went on, I must tell you that I thought of you every second . . . here was a man who lay down his life for me. God almighty, Jack, do you know how wonderful that is?' He had stayed silent, and she added, softly, 'No, you don't do you?' She gave his ear a gentle kiss before she walked back to hold her Emilio's hand. She was fighting back tears and losing the struggle.

Jack turned his mare and off they went, slow and steady, with both men working hard to keep the wounds of the fight out of their minds. They were patched up, over the small cuts and bruises, but there were things that could not be healed, deep down.

They were leaving a battlefield, and one battlefield looks very much like any other. There were dead men and dead horses; there were men bleeding and moaning, being carried away to be healed and comforted; there were priests and medical men treading around the fields, and most of all there was a smell of death, and that took a while to go. Some men had run for their lives and some had stood their ground. Some few had won honours and more than a few had done deeds that would be stories to tell when they were old.

'How the hell did we come out of that with body and soul held together, Brady? Look at it . . . Laredo!

153

We're in for some bad dreams.'

'We held it together because the animal came out. The teeth were bared and we faced the hunters. Am I right?'

'You usually are.'

But for Jack Brady, who paused for a minute as he swung his mare around and looked back, the fight outside Laredo had maybe been his last chance to prove to his father that he could do something to be remembered for. He had made a mark.

'Are you watching me from up there, Pa? Maybe Pastor Jim sits with you. Well I think I won some honour out there. You know what I learned, Wate? I learned that when it comes to honour, no money can buy it.'

'Well I could have told you that!'

'Sure – you great bag of hot air. Truth is, I never knew honour was worth the trouble.

'Now I know different.'

15

The great theatre of war, as the generals would call it, sitting at their meetings after Laredo, could be anywhere on earth. An army had to fight in a desert or along a mountain chain; in a canyon or across a great plain. The challenge was the same: victory or defeat, honour or shame. But unlike the generals, the men fighting in the middle of the hell of battle forgot the terrain and remembered the pains of the day. In Laredo, those pains went on, over the time the place changed hands from Mexican to American, and only when things were settled did it stay put, wrenched away from General Arista. Jack and Wate had played a part in securing that town, and it was a part of the history of their time. Yet neither thought of these things as they jogged on north, taking in the sense of that endless beauty: both awesome and terrifying.

The borderlands were broad and deep enough to hold and hide any number of men running from the law, or from danger, or even from their past. It was deep enough to hide Jack and Wate as they pointed north-east and tried not to think of tomorrow. Striking out into the stone and sand, and the great plateau reaching out eventually into Comancheria where the margins of settled life ended, was a liberating experience. It opened out a man's thoughts to anything, any dreams and fancies.

Never had the southern tracts of wasteland territory looked so immense to Jack, who had ridden over most of the earth between the Choctaw land by Arkansas and the Pawnee by the Platte river. He was no more than a scrawny kid when he had first run away through Illinois and Missouri. Great open space had always called to him, and he had always been running from something. Now here he was, feeling better by doing something to be remembered by, but still with a bad label – he was a deserter. But he felt so good that he had rubbed out any remains of conscience. In his heart, he had proved himself, so that the father hanging onto his weaknesses inside would now let him go. Only he knew he was a deserter: the Spekes would make it plain that he died on the field.

Jesus, he thought to himself, *maybe there'll be some kind of record . . . on a paper somewhere, there'll be my name on the list of those who died for the cause of the*

United States and Texas . . . hell, another damned lie.

He had to tell Wate, but the man laughed it off, as always. 'Come on . . . even if there is your name up in marble, Brady, with the glorious dead, it's sort of right. I mean, didn't some part of you die back there?'

Hell, the man was right. Jack saw the truth of what he had done. Yes, the old Jack died in Laredo, and it was the last chance of the new Jack. He had taken that last chance. Maybe some men don't get that chance at all. These thoughts came through him like a cool breeze in a hot summer.

Evan Wate, troubled by nothing except the rumble of his empty stomach, looked at Jack and chuckled to himself. He had seldom seen a man who had so much turmoil down there inside. Shame the poor man hadn't no stomach to bother him instead of the conscience.

Jack's mind was slowly losing the edge of fear and excitement that had put his life so close to death that he could smell his grave. Now he was allowing himself to think with some elbow room, to imagine a new place and some new smells, new footprints. Evan Wate was still confused and baffled as to how he had come through that fight with Herrera. It was unreal, yet it did happen, and yes, he was still alive.

The two riders were heading north, passing Callego, and both were thinking of the first time they had stopped there. But now they were riding to

157

whatever place they could call home. Jack Brady was lower in the saddle, but then almost everyone west of Topeka was shorter than Evan Wate, who rode alongside.

'You bring to mind the bar in that place, Brady? We had a run-in.' Wate asked.

'How could I forget? You got the drop on me. You have an unfair height advantage.'

'I don't know. I think you hold your own pretty well.'

'Now, big man, I'd like to think, after what we been through, that we could be *amigos*. What do you say?'

Evan Wate managed to smile, ever so slightly creasing his face. 'Now that might be difficult because you see . . . well, put it this way. Do you recall a small town called Nelland, Louisiana?'

'Nope. I seen so many small towns.'

'Well maybe you recall a girl named Marie?' Wate asked, real slow, as if it was a torment.

'Come on . . . that's the commonest woman's name this side of the Rio Grande . . . and I know because I've seen the Rio Grande now!'

They shared the joke, and cantered on, going north and with their hearts full of hope. For Evan Wate, the destination was any one of a string of towns where he had some kin, and he had some tales to tell.

They split, with Evan Wate pointing his mount east to Louisiana, and Jack Brady riding north over the Red River. 'Surely our paths will cross again, Jack Brady,' Wate said, as they shook hands, as they had done before, now good friends for life. 'Yeah . . . you and me . . . we ride so much, we're so restless, that we'll meet up, you bet!' Jack said.

As for Jack Brady, he was aiming to call in at Short Bend and tell Mosey Digby that he should find more work for any stray padres he might know. But too bad that Pastor Jim was not available for prayers and advice.

There was one last job to be done, at the first place where he could leave a letter with a stage. This was to do what Jim had asked him to do: Pastor Jim, the man who had talked him into the adventure he had just survived. Jack never had a chance to tell the man what he owed him, but he could do this one good thing for the man who had more than likely saved his life that day by the Rio Grande. He passed close to Fort Gibson, and there he left a letter addressed to Bullhead at San Antonio. He would be told that Emilio and Liza were well and were at Laredo. He decided not to mention that his friend Pastor Jim had died while disposing of a number of Mexicans, and so breaking any vow he might have made to his God.

Jack Brady had done something of which even his father would approve. Yes, something memorable, something that made folk remember him for the right reasons. Now he turned his thoughts towards

Kansas, just because of all the places he had worked, that was one where plenty of folks got together to ride west, and after what he had been through, the paths west presented nothing that smacked of fear. He could face anything.